FROM: URNEWREALITY
TO: NATTYNED145
UNR KNOWS ALL ABOUT U. UNR THINKS U SHOULD CHECK
OUT THE ATTACHMENT. UNR NEEDS A FAVOR. . . . IF U
DON'T WANT EVERY1 TO KNOW ABOUT THE ATTACHED . . .
U WILL BE READY TO HELP WHEN UNR SENDS DETAILS. . . .

I frowned. *If u don't want every1 to know about the attached* . . . This was a blackmail message. Just like the message Shannon had received. UrNewReality was trying to control the people who knew me, trying to get them to—what? What could UrNewReality believe my boyfriend would do to me?

NANCY DREW

Available from Aladdin Paperbacks

CAROLYN KEENE

NANCY DREW

GIRL DETECTIVE®

Identity Revealed

#35

**Book Three in the
Identity Mystery Trilogy**

Aladdin Paperbacks
New York   London   Toronto   Sydney

This book is a work of fiction. Any references to historical events, real people, or real locales are used fictitiously. Other names, characters, places, and incidents are the product of the author's imagination, and any resemblance to actual events or locales or persons, living or dead, is entirely coincidental.

❧ ALADDIN PAPERBACKS
An imprint of Simon & Schuster Children's Publishing Division
1230 Avenue of the Americas, New York, NY 10020
Copyright © 2009 by Simon & Schuster, Inc.
All rights reserved, including the right of
reproduction in whole or in part in any form.
NANCY DREW, NANCY DREW: GIRL DETECTIVE, ALADDIN PAPER-
BACKS, and related logo are registered trademarks of Simon & Schuster, Inc.
Manufactured in the United States of America
10 9 8 7 6 5
Library of Congress Control Number 2008922948
ISBN-13: 978-1-4169-6828-3
ISBN-10: 1-4169-6828-8
0412 OFF

Contents

IDENTITY REVEALED

A SERIOUS LEAK

"This is a potential disaster, Nancy," my father said gravely, shaking his head as if he couldn't quite believe it.

"I'm so sorry, Dad," I replied honestly. We were sitting in our living room surrounded by my best friends, Bess and George, and my boyfriend, Ned Nickerson. Ned and I had just been on a long-awaited date—we were finally getting a chance to catch up after a case had brought me to New York, and another one had distracted me right here in River Heights. But then a phone call from George had interrupted our romantic moment. It turned out there was a huge development in the case I'd been working on *here*—a development that could be a huge setback for my father, and that made me feel guiltier than I could even express.

"I had no idea that someone could have the capability to access your files, much less post them on the Internet," I went on.

My dad sighed, glancing down at the glowing screen of George's laptop. There, scans of files relating to a huge case Dad was working on winked out at us, seeming to mock our every move. George had interrupted my date with Ned to tell me that I needed to log on to BetterLife, an incredibly popular virtual reality/networking game on the Web that I'd been noodling around in for my latest case. There, I'd found a message waiting for my avatar, VirtualNancy. It had read simply MYOB—OR ELSE—and attached were these scans of my father's confidential files relating to his case.

I wish I could say that being cyberharassed was new to me, but unfortunately this case had shown me all the dark and creepy aspects of cybercommunication. Until this message, though, I thought we'd finally found the person who'd been using my BetterLife and e-mail accounts to make my real life as difficult as possible. With this message, everything changed. The woman I'd thought was the culprit was behind bars with no access to BetterLife. And *somebody* was still out there, trying to use their computer to take me down.

"At least the police are looking into it," Ned volunteered gently. He caught my eye and gave me a tentative little smile, like he was trying to cheer me up. I tried to smile back, but it was hard—the police had just left after discussing the whole situation with us, but they hadn't exactly inspired a lot of confidence in their computer abilities.

"Too bad they'd never heard of BetterLife," George muttered, an edge of disbelief still coloring her voice. George is my personal computer guru—anything that has keys and a screen, she understands completely. I think she was personally offended by the policemen's lack of technosavvy.

"There is one bright spot," my dad continued with a sigh, settling back in his easy chair. "As I told the police, these files don't *directly* relate to our case. They're all affidavits and interviews relating to a line of defense we decided not to pursue. So they wouldn't necessarily destroy our case if they were released." He paused. "Although the very fact that someone accessed them concerns me greatly."

"That's what I don't understand," I piped in. "Whoever's doing this has access to my computer, okay. And he or she seems to know everything about me—so it wouldn't be that hard to figure out that you're my father, or that I might have something to lose if your files were released. But how did e-mail or BetterLife make it possible for someone to access your private files? The two aren't related."

Instinctively, we all turned to George.

"Well," George began, looking a little overwhelmed. "I don't know *exactly* how they're doing it, but I can give you a basic idea. You guys all send e-mails, right?"

"Right," we all chorused. George glanced over at my dad, looking like she wasn't entirely convinced.

"Right," he insisted, a smile creeping at the edges of his lips. "I'm not from the Stone Age, you know."

George shrugged. "Okay. So you've all seen the headers that come on e-mails—the long number that appears next to the sender and receiver's address?"

Bess frowned. "I guess," she replied. "What is that number, anyway? It doesn't seem to have anything to do with the rest of the info."

George nodded. "That's the IP address. Every computer that connects to the Internet has one. It's what web merchants use to track who's visiting their site, and it's the reason eBay or Amazon or your bank's website are able to identify you when you bring up their site. When they see your IP address, they know they're dealing with, say, Nancy Drew at her home computer."

I nodded slowly. "Huh," I muttered.

"In theory," George went on, looking a little more perplexed, "websites could use that address to get more information from your computer. Most operating systems have firewalls to block that, though—to keep random hackers from using the Internet to get access to your files." She paused. "It seems like whoever's behind this has found a way around those firewalls. Which means he or she is a pretty advanced hacker, indeed."

My father was frowning and tapping his chin, trying to make sense of all this technobabble, I guess. "Wait a minute, George," he interjected after a moment. "You said they could access *computer* files that way. But actually, these files weren't stored on the computer—they were hard copies, kept in a traditional file. You know, with a folder and a cabinet and all that." He cleared his throat. "A *real* folder. Manila."

George furrowed her brows. "A *real* folder?" she asked. "So you mean these didn't originate as files—someone took your actual papers and scanned them?"

Dad seemed to be thinking, and suddenly leapt to his feet. We all followed him through the living room, down the hall, and into his home office. There, he purposely strode over to a filing cabinet and pulled it open. After sifting through some files, Dad reached in and pulled out a manila folder. He opened it with a flourish, exposing four or five pieces of paper.

"Correction," he said, licking his finger and separating the pages. "Someone accessed my files, took my papers, scanned them—and then returned them."

Hmmmm. I turned this over in my brain, trying to make sense of it. Who would be able to not only grab the files, but give them *back*? Without being noticed? Was there anyone who worked for Dad . . . ?

"Dad," I began. "Last week when you were swamped, I helped out in the office. But I know you've had a ton of work to get through and I haven't been here twenty-four–seven. Have you had anyone else come in to help you with your filing?"

Dad was still flipping through his papers, looking as confused by this as I felt. "Actually," he replied, "I did, once. It was the night you were babysitting. Rosanne, my secretary, recommended two girls from her neighborhood, and they came in to file. These girls were so young, though— barely teenagers! They wouldn't have known what to do with those—"

"What were their names?" Bess interrupted. I turned to catch her eye, and knew she was thinking exactly what I was.

My father frowned, obviously trying to recall. "Shannon," he said after a moment. "And something that begins with *R*. Rosie? Rachel?"

I glanced at Bess and George. They looked as incredulous as I felt. Shannon and Rebecca, the only two pre-teenage girls on the face of the earth that I might think capable of this.

I fished my car keys out of my pocket. "Excuse me," I said, turning to my dad and Ned. "But I think Bess, George, and I have somebody we need to question."

LAX PUNISHMENTS

"So Shannon and Rebecca are still friends, huh?" Bess asked as she buckled into the passenger seat of my Prius. George settled herself in the back seat as I turned the key in the ignition and started backing down our driveway.

"Amazingly, it seems like they are," I replied, shaking my head in disbelief. Shannon Fitzgerald, a classmate of Bess's little sister Maggie, was the reason I had gotten involved in the whole BetterLife world to begin with. A couple weeks ago, Maggie told me that a friend of hers was being harassed via e-mail and BetterLife—and that it had gotten so bad, her friend was even missing school. That friend was Shannon Fitzgerald, and

I soon learned that what Maggie claimed was true: Shannon—or at least her BetterLife incarnation, SassyGirl48—was being seriously bullied and verbally abused online. After a few days of sleuthing, I realized that it was Shannon's so-called best friend, Rebecca, who had instigated the bullying—and *she* claimed she was just getting Shannon back for a lifetime of real-life bullying, of her and of nearly everyone else in their class.

"I can't imagine making up with someone who had caused me so much distress," Bess muttered. "I mean, basically they each tried to ruin the other's life."

"And all over a boy," George said, tsk-tsking.

In the course of my investigation, I'd learned that the whole Shannon–Rebecca conflict had been set in motion by one mutually-crushed-on fifteen-year-old hottie named Jake.

I shrugged. "Well, they're back together now," I said, turning onto Shannon's street.

Bess grinned. "You know what they say," she said, turning to give each of us a saucy look. "Sis-tahs before mistahs."

George and I groaned. "Please never say that again," George begged.

"Seriously though," I began, trying to change

the subject. "Rebecca and Shannon are grounded. They're not supposed to go anywhere near a computer for another month or so. So how would they have scanned and posted those files?"

George shrugged. "They had to have used a computer," she replied. "Is there any chance they're cheating on their grounding?"

"There's always a chance," I replied, honestly. One thing I've learned from sleuthing is that *anyone* is capable of *anything*; you can't assume you know what decisions a person would make without knowing them really, really well. And even then you can be wrong. "Still, though," I went on, thinking aloud. "I talked to Shannon just last week, asking about her aunt." Shannon's aunt Agnes had been involved in some seriously shady business . . . in fact, *she* was the person I'd believed responsible for all the cyberharassment I'd experienced after solving Shannon's case. Now that I'd received this new e-mail with scans of Dad's files, though, I knew she wasn't behind it all. "Shannon seemed totally bored. I really believed she hadn't been near a computer in weeks."

"Weird, then," George murmured.

We'd arrived at Rebecca's house, forcing our conversation to an end. I parked the car on the street outside, opened my door, and hopped out.

"All right, ladies." I shoved my keys in my pocket and nodded at my friends with a determined expression. "Let's get to the bottom of this."

We strolled up to Rebecca's front door and I pushed the doorbell. As we waited there for someone to answer, I wasn't sure what to hope for. Would it be better for the girls to have broken their punishments and posted the files, just to have a culprit in hand? Or would that totally shatter my faith in these girls, who really did seem like decent people at heart?

"Hello?" A middle-aged woman I recognized as Rebecca's mother opened the door a tiny bit and poked her head out. "Can I help you? Aren't you—Nancy, isn't it?"

I nodded and explained that we were looking for Shannon and Rebecca. Nothing to get upset about (*yet*, I thought to myself); we just needed to ask them some questions.

"Oh, dear," Rebecca's mom murmured, shaking her head. "Well, I'm afraid she's not here. Rebecca and Shannon have been doing so well with their punishments, we decided to let them have a supervised sleepover at the Fitzgeralds' house."

"Oh." I just stood there for a moment, stunned by this new information. A *sleepover*? Just a couple weeks after Rebecca had basically instigated a cyberwitchhunt on the very friend at whose house she was sleeping over? "Um . . . okay. I guess we'll just look for her there."

With a confused glance at my friends, I led them back to the car.

"Wow," I muttered, climbing back into the driver's seat.

"Yeah, wow," George echoed. "Okay, what would Rebecca have had to do to seriously get grounded for a month? Because the last time I checked, you don't have sleepovers when you're grounded."

Bess shook her head. "Two weeks," she said with a sigh. "That's how long her parents held out? I wish my parents had been that easy."

"To be fair," George cut in, "maybe their not being that easy has something to do with your not being a bully who harasses people over the Internet."

I frowned at George in the rearview mirror. "Girls, girls," I cautioned, "let's not jump to conclusions. Maybe Rebecca and Shannon really were being little angels, and deserved a sleepover to let off some steam."

George snorted. "Ha. I'll believe that when I see it."

It took about five minutes to drive from Rebecca's house to Shannon's. After parking the car in the driveway, we strode up to the front door and knocked. It only took a few seconds for Shannon's mother, Mrs. Fitzgerald, to come to the door, and when she spotted me she looked less than thrilled.

"Nancy," she said cautiously, opening the door with nervous glances at Bess and George behind me. "Well. What a . . . surprise. I certainly hope—"

"Mrs. Fitzgerald, let me put your mind at rest," I cut in, softening my voice. "We're not here because Shannon's done anything wrong. Something just came up in a different case I'm working on, and I need to ask her and Rebecca some questions."

"Oh," Mrs. Fitzgerald replied, relief spreading over her face. "Oh. Well, that's fine, then. Rebecca and Shannon are actually doing quite well with their punishments, so we've let them have a sleepover." She stepped back and opened the door for us, leading us into the foyer.

"So we heard," George murmured, slipping past her.

"We worked together with Rebecca's parents to come up with an effective punishment," Mrs.

Fitzgerald went on. "You know, bullying is a terrible thing, but cyberbullying! Who in my generation had even heard of it? We decided to ground them not just from computers, but from all electronic devices."

I nodded. "Wow. That's intense."

Mrs. Fitzgerald smiled. "Yes. But we wanted to make sure they learned their lesson! I think they've been going a little stir-crazy with no computer, no television, no cell phone, and no iPod," she went on. "They've had to rediscover books and letter-writing! And they've been meeting with a counselor, you know, separately, to talk about their issues."

I smiled. "That all sounds great."

Mrs. Fitzgerald nodded. "Yes, yes." She shook her head, as if shaking off an idea. "Look at me, keeping you trapped in our hallway while I tell you all about their punishments. You said you wanted to speak to the girls. Here, follow me."

I knew the way to Shannon's room—I'd questioned her plenty of times when I was working on her cyber-bullying case—but I fell into step behind Mrs. Fitzgerald anyway, and followed her up the white-carpeted stairs. I sensed that she was nervous. The last few times I'd come to visit, I hadn't brought good news. And I really hoped that this time would be different, and that Shannon and Rebecca would turn out to be the little angels their parents thought they were.

We reached the door to Shannon's room, which was eerily silent. No music, no television, not even any voices could be heard within. Mrs. Fitzgerald knocked gently on the door with the back of her hand. "Girls?" she called softly. Then she gripped the doorknob and opened the door wide, calling in, "There are some people here to speak with you. . . ."

There they were: Shannon and Rebecca. They were huddled on the floor, their backs to us, their shoulders hunched to hide whatever they were working with.

"*Mooooom!*" Shannon whined, looking horrified. "When you knock, you're supposed to wait for us to answer!"

Rebecca dived to the floor, moving quickly to pick something up. But she was too late. We'd all had a clear view of what they'd been dealing with. With a gulp, I glanced at Bess and George and slowly shook my head.

George met my eye. "Oh. My. God," she said simply.

VIRTUAL SECRETS

Shannon's bedroom floor was covered with Barbies.

"We were just *sorting*," Shannon insisted, turning from her mother to George, Bess, and me. "I found some old toys in my closet, so Rebecca and I were just going through them so we could give them to charity or something! I mean, I am *way* too old to still play with the silly things. We just wanted to—brush their hair before we give them to some poor unsuspecting child."

I couldn't help but notice, as Shannon explained all this, that the Barbies seemed to be all dressed up in evening gowns, and that there was a tiny sign that read THE ACADEMY AWARDS taped onto a cardboard box that seemed to be serving as a makeshift podium.

Mrs. Fitzgerald looked delighted. "There's nothing to be ashamed of, Shannon," she said, reaching out to stroke her daughter's long blond hair. "Why, I used to love playing Barbies when I was a girl! And isn't playing with your dolls more fun than living some imaginary life on whozit dot com?"

Shannon ducked away from her mother, her face bright red. "*Mother*," she insisted. "We were *sorting*. Gosh, you never listen!"

"A-hem," I broke in, clearing my throat. "Not to interrupt, but if you can stop sorting for a few minutes, I had some questions to ask you girls."

Shannon glanced from her mom to me, and Rebecca looked up from the floor, where she was rapidly shoving the glammed-up Barbies into a shoebox. It was like both girls were noticing me for the first time: I watched their expressions go from embarrassment to confusion and dread. After our last few visits had ended with groundings and counselors, I'm sure they were wondering what questions I could possibly have for them now.

"I'll just leave you alone," Mrs. Fitzgerald announced, with one last nervous glance at me. "If there's anything I can do," she told me, lowering her voice. "Or Mr. Fitzgerald—anything at all— we'll be downstairs."

I gave her what I hoped was a reassuring smile. "This shouldn't take long."

She nodded and slipped out the door, closing it behind her.

"What are you doing here?" Shannon asked me as soon as her mother was gone, in a not-entirely- friendly tone. She and Rebecca were both watch- ing me suspiciously now, their lips curling with annoyance. Oh well. I hadn't expected them to be happy to see me.

"I have some questions for you," I replied casu- ally, walking over to Shannon's pink-covered bed and taking a seat. "And before I start, I want to stress that you guys aren't in trouble, okay? But I need you to be completely honest with me. This is serious, and I need to figure out what's really going on."

Rebecca frowned, and she and Shannon ex- changed a quick, curious glance. Shannon nodded at her friend almost imperceptibly, then turned to me.

"Okay," she said in a resigned tone. "Shoot. Let's get this over with."

I nodded. "Right. Well, I know you guys haven't been on BetterLife in a while."

Rebecca looked stung, like just my mention of the popular online game hurt. "Um, *no*. Thanks to you, all we do now is sit around and dress up Barbies."

Shannon glared at her friend. "Re-*becca*!"

Rebecca gulped. "I mean, design clothes for them. Or sort them to give away. Whatever."

I nodded again. "Okay. But today, I got a pretty disturbing message on BetterLife. It said I'd better learn to mind my own business—and it had copies of some very confidential files of my father's attached."

Both girls stared at me blankly. "What, embarrassing e-mails or something?" Shannon asked.

George chuckled. "No," she replied. I had to admit, though, the thought of my dad sending e-mails dogging his BFF or something was fairly amusing. "Nancy's dad is a lawyer," she explained. "These were files having to do with a very important case he has coming up."

"They're files that *nobody* should see before the trial," Bess added ominously. "Files that, if they were released to the public, could ruin months and months of his hard work."

Shannon and Rebecca glanced at each other, seeming to absorb this information. I tried to read their expressions for any sign that they knew what we were talking about, but saw none.

"Okay," Rebecca said finally, in a cautious tone. "And this brought you to us—why?"

Shannon swallowed and flipped her hair, fixing on me with a petulant expression. "I don't know if you picked this up, but we're *twelve*," she told me, shaking her head a little. "We don't know anything about your lawyer dad or his big dumb case."

I bit my lip. Normally, when you question someone and they suddenly turn nasty, that implies they're uncomfortable with the line of questioning and might have something to hide. With Shannon, though, it was just par for the course.

"The message was from Guitarlvr15," I replied. "Rebecca's old avatar."

Shannon and Rebecca exchanged glances that I couldn't quite read.

"That's really weird," Rebecca said finally, looking me in the eye. "Because I haven't touched Guitarlvr15 or anything having to do with a computer since I got grounded."

"My father said he had some help in his office last week," I added. "Some girls your age. When he described them, they sounded a whole lot like you."

Shannon swallowed, and turned to glance at Rebecca.

"It was," Rebecca replied, breezily. "I mean, probably. One of our neighbors asked us to help her boss, some big lawyer guy, with his files last week. We were just being nice. I mean, he just gave us a few bucks and free pizza."

"Which wasn't even good," Shannon added, turning to me with a piercing glare. "Who eats pepperoni?"

Rebecca shook her head. "*Anyway*," she went on, "we didn't even know the guy was your dad. Why would we have stolen his files?"

I just looked at Rebecca, considering. Yup, that was definitely the big hole in my theory—why would they have done it?

"To get back at me?" I theorized. "When I told your parents what you'd done on BetterLife, you got in a lot of trouble. I know from talking to Shannon last week that things haven't been fun for you guys since you got grounded. Maybe you took my dad's files as a harmless prank to show me who's boss—maybe you didn't even realize how important they were."

Shannon pursed her lips and shook her head, looking like she was bored of this whole conversation. (Which really said something, considering how bored they supposedly were when we came in.) "We didn't even *know* that lawyer guy was your dad," she insisted. "I mean, yeah, you're not our BFF or anything, but that's just way too much energy to put into ruining your life," she went on. "No offense."

"Besides," Rebecca piped up, looking like she had just thought of something, "how would we have scanned them or posted them online? We have no computer access, remember?"

I glanced over at George. She shrugged like they had a point. If they really weren't accessing the Internet, how could they have done it?

"And you're really telling us the truth here?" I pressed. "You're not sneaking on to computers at school or anything? You can tell me."

Shannon rolled her eyes. "Only when we have to for computer science," she replied. "We're building a class web page, which is *totally* boring. Other than that—no."

I looked from Shannon to Rebecca. Their faces both seemed totally open and sincere, if bored with this conversation and ready for us to leave so they could get back to what they were doing. I couldn't help but sigh. If Shannon and Rebecca weren't behind the e-mail with my dad's files attached, who was? Who would care that much about showing me who was (virtual) boss?

Reluctantly, I got to my feet. "All right, girls," I said with an apologetic shrug. "Sorry to waste your time."

I nodded to Bess and George, who also stood to go, both looking as disappointed as I felt. We began shuffling toward the door. Just as Rebecca and Shannon were looking from our retreating forms back to each other, a loud *BLOOOOOOP* sounded.

"What on earth?" Bess asked, turning to George. It sounded like the *BLOOOOOP* had come from her jeans. "Are *you* electronic now?"

George just smiled and fished a small black square out of her pocket. "It's my PDA," she replied. "I have an e-mail." Pressing a button, she brought the screen to life and frowned at the display. "That's weird," she said, shooting me a meaningful glance. "It's from Ned. And the subject is 'Important!'"

That was odd. "Open it!" I replied. "Ned doesn't fool around with that word."

George made a series of clicks and scrolls. Soon whatever the e-mail contained lit up her screen—and George's eyes widened.

"Whoa," she breathed. "Uh, Nance—you'll want to take a look at this."

Without another word, George passed me her PDA. I grabbed it, then turned it right side up, and then read:

TO: NOTABOY@FASTMAIL.COM
FROM: NATTYNED48@RHU.EDU
SUBJECT: IMPORTANT! LOOK RIGHT AWAY!
GIRLS—
WONDERING WHO COULD BE BEHIND THESE E-MAILS, I
DECIDED TO DO SOME SLEUTHING OF MY OWN—ON
BETTERLIFE. YOU'LL WANT TO CHECK OUT THE ATTACHED
PAGE. BE CAREFUL, NED.

Hmmmm. I scrolled down to view the attachment. It appeared to be a screenshot from a message board from the BetterLife community. All of the messages were replies to one posting under the subject SHE'S BAAAACK: BLONDIE86, R U SHANNON?

I skimmed through the postings.

SHE HAS BLOND HAIR, AND SHE JUST TOLD ME HER
FAVORITE BAND IS BLUE MONDAY. WE KNOW SHANNON
LUUURVES THEM. . . .
. . . SHE WAS OFFLINE FOR EXACTLY FORTY-FIVE
MINUTES LAST NIGHT, RIGHT WHEN SHANNON HAS HER
PIANO LESSON. . . .

. . . SHE PLAYS THE GAME EXACTLY LIKE SHANNON DID WITH SASSYGIRL48: FIRST SHE'S A JANITOR, THEN A BOOKSTORE MANAGER, PLUS SHE DRESSES ALMOST EXACTLY THE SAME. . . .

The discussion thread ended with a final posting entitled U GOT ME.

POSTED BY: BLONDIE86
ALRIGHT U FOUND ME OUT BABEEZ! IT'S ME—UR FAVORITE BLONDIE! KEEP IT ON THE DL THO—YOU CANNOT TELL MY PARENTS!
SHANNON

I looked to George. Could it be real—could Shannon have just lied to us about being back on BetterLife, or being near a computer at all? She frowned. "Yup. It means exactly what you think it means," she said, turning to Shannon. "You were lying when you said you haven't been on BetterLife since you were grounded! You've been posting this whole time—under your new username, Blondie86."

Shannon looked stunned. After a moment, her face fell. She looked nervously to Rebecca, but her friend looked just as crestfallen as she was.

"Just tell us the truth," I urged them. "We're

not here to punish you. I just need to get to the bottom of this."

Shannon looked down at her lap, then quietly spoke. "Okay," she said, and got up from the bed and walked over to her closet. Without another word, she opened it up and pulled out a purple backpack. She placed the backpack on the floor, opened the top, and carefully pulled out a huge, beat-up–looking laptop. PROPERTY OF RHMS was stamped on the top.

"You can't tell my parents," Shannon pleaded, looking up at us for the first time.

I shook my head slowly. "You know I can't promise that, Shannon."

"Just tell us what's going on," Bess coaxed from behind me. "We already have a fair idea. Tell us whether you're behind the e-mail with the files."

Shannon sighed and brought the laptop over to her bed. Slowly, Rebecca got up and stood near her friend as Shannon opened the computer and powered it up.

"It's from my computer science teacher," Shannon explained. "I told her I needed it to work on the class web page outside school. I told her we didn't have a family computer—not that I was grounded."

I nodded. "Okay. Why did you do that?"

Shannon's eyes flashed angrily. "I was *so* bored!" she cried. "You don't know what it's like—you're so much older. For us, though, so much of talking to our friends and keeping up with each other is online! Without a computer, I felt like a total outcast. I didn't even know what my friends were talking about half the time, because I couldn't get on BetterLife."

Rebecca nodded. "It just didn't seem fair," she added. "I mean, I'm sure our parents thought taking away our computers would be like taking away TV or phone privileges. It would be tough, but we'd be fine without it. But being online means so much more to us than it does to them! Without BetterLife, I felt like less of *myself.*"

I glanced at George. I was sure the alarm I saw in her eyes was present in mine. Less of *myself?* Because they couldn't play a computer game?

"So I lied to my teacher," Shannon went on. As she explained, her laptop became available and she double-clicked on the Internet browser, then entered the BetterLife URL. "I didn't want to. I *had* to. I needed to be able to see my friends, not just at school, but—"

"In this virtual world," George supplied, her voice sounding as though she couldn't quite believe what she was saying.

"Right," Shannon agreed sheepishly. The login screen for BetterLife was up, and she quickly typed in "Blondie86" and a password my eyes weren't fast enough to catch. Immediately, the game loaded and we came up on a young blond girl sitting on a park bench, reading the newspaper.

"Wait a minute," I cried, pointing. "I recognize this character! She was protesting Virtual-Nancy earlier."

I looked to Shannon; she just shrugged and glanced at Rebecca. "Blondie86 might have been there," she agreed, turning back to the screen. Her voice dropped. "It was *cold* what you did to that boy."

"I didn't—" I started to defend VirtualNancy, then stopped. It wasn't worth it. As part of my cyberharassment, someone had hacked into my BetterLife account and made it look like Virtu-alNancy was making racist slurs against one of my real-life friends, Ibrahim. Video of my avatar doing this were then uploaded to uVid, a related site where BetterLife users can share moments from the game with other players. VirtualNancy got lots of attention from her fellow players after that—mostly negative.

Shannon was staring at the screen. YOU HAVE

1 NEW MESSAGE, it read. She clicked on the envelope icon that brought you to messages left for your character.

There was only one message in her in-box. The subject was STAY TUNED. And the sender was UrNewReality.

"Wait!" I cried, pointing at the screen again. "UrNewReality. The person who sent that message. Have you gotten messages from that person before?"

UrNewReality was no stranger to me or VirtualNancy. I'd gotten several messages from him or her over the last week or so, all threatening. UrNewReality was not one of my biggest fans.

Shannon gulped and looked at Rebecca again. Then she looked up at me, and her expression was sincere. "I'm really sorry."

"What do you mean?" I asked, drawing closer.

In response, she turned back to the computer and clicked on another message. "I got this a week ago. A few days after I created Blondie86."

I looked at the screen.

FROM: URNEWREALITY
TO: BLONDIE86
SUBJECT: UR NEW REALITY
UNR KNOWS WHO U REALLY R. UNR KNOWS WHO CAN'T

KNOW. UNR NEEDS A FAVOR, AND U WILL COME THRU,
OR UNR WILL TELL UR PARENTS THE TRUTH ABOUT U.

I looked up at Shannon, stunned.

"I didn't want to do anything wrong," Shannon explained. "Really. I mean, I knew I was going against my punishment by being on the computer at all, but I really just wanted to talk to my friends. Hang out with them online. Have a little fun." She cringed. "But I really didn't want my parents to know. I didn't want to get in trouble again and get grounded even worse. So a couple days later, when UrNewReality contacted me again . . ."

I couldn't believe it. "What did he ask you to do?" I asked.

Shannon sighed. "He—or she. I don't know," she explained. "He wanted me to chat up my neighbor, Mrs. Fultz, who works for your father. I didn't know why. He just wanted me to say that Rebecca and I were looking to make a little money this summer, and did she know about any odd jobs? That's when Mrs. Fultz told me that your dad needed some help filing."

I nodded. This was completely blowing my mind. How had UrNewReality known my father's office was overloaded with filing, or that Mrs.

Fultz was Shannon's neighbor? And why did the final message to me come from Guitarlvr15? Were there two cyberbullies working together, or were the two avatars being used to confuse me?

"So we went and worked for your dad one night," Rebecca took over. "It was totally boring: filing and pizza. But before we left, Shannon got one last message: We were supposed to steal some papers from your dad's confidential files while we were there, scan them at school, and then put the hard copies back."

Shannon nodded. "We did it, and I snuck them back into the files when we went to pick up our pay."

I glanced at Bess and George. Their expressions seemed to say exactly what I was thinking: *Whoa.*

"And the files?" I said finally, after processing all this. "The computer files, I mean? Did you send them to . . . Guitarlvr15?"

Shannon frowned and shook her head. "No. That would have seemed pretty weird. We didn't even know there was another Guitarlvr15 online. A few days after we did this, I got a message from UrNewReality with an e-mail address I should send the files to," Shannon explained. "So I did. I thought after we did this, we'd be done, but

UrNewReality keeps sending me messages that say I should 'stay tuned' . . . for his next instructions, I guess."

I shook my head, trying to make sense of it all.

"What was the e-mail address?" George asked, her head tilted pensively.

Shannon made a couple of clicks on the laptop to bring up the message. "Someone at anonymous dot com," she replied. "A weird one. I've never heard of that e-mail service before."

George nodded, looking disappointed. "They specialize in anonymous messages," she murmured with a sigh. "Those addresses are basically impossible to track."

I was still trying to figure out what all of this meant. "So you did it," I began, "but you didn't *really*. Or you did it, but you didn't know why. UrNewReality is really the person behind this. You don't know anything about Guitarlvr15's involvement. Is that it?"

Rebecca nodded furiously. "That's it," she said. "We were just innocent people being blackmailed into helping!"

"And this isn't, like, a two-weeks-ago situation," Bess suggested, "where you tell us over and over that you don't know who's sending the messages, and then it turns out to be you?"

Rebecca gulped. "I swear to you," she replied, holding up her left hand in something that looked like the Girl Scout symbol, "I have no idea who UrNewReality is."

"I was being honest about one thing before," Shannon added, nodding supportively. "I really would not put this much energy into ruining your life."

I sighed. Bluntly spoken, another dead end.

After a few seconds of biting my lip and running over it all again in my head, I became aware that Rebecca and Shannon were still staring at me. Staring at me *imploringly*. Maybe even *desperately*.

"What?" I asked, already thinking ahead to who we'd question next.

Shannon gave me a pleading look. "Are you going to tell our parents?" she asked.

"We'll do anything you say," Rebecca added. "We'll throw away our computers! We'll even help you find this NewReality guy! Just *please*—"

I held up my hand. "Girls," I said, "you know I have to. I can't lie to your parents."

Now totally crestfallen, the girls turned to each other with utterly hopeless expressions. After a few seconds, Shannon started to sniffle.

"Come on, everyone," I said with a sigh, beckoning the girls, Bess, and George into the hallway to find the Fitzgeralds. "I hate to say it, but it looks like this is going to be another long night."

CREEPY CHARACTERS

"Okay," George announced, as she, Bess and I settled in front of my computer the next morning. "I guess it's official; UrNewReality definitely wasn't Agnes. And he's definitely still out there, causing trouble."

Bess and I nodded grimly. It was true; I'd hoped the threatening messages I'd been getting for a while now—the same kind of messages Shannon had received—had been coming from her crazy Aunt Agnes. But now Agnes was behind bars with no computer access, and the cyberharassment continued.

"Let's get to the bottom of this," Bess announced with a determined expression.

I'd invited them both over so we could get back on BetterLife. This time, though, we weren't playing with our existing character, Dancin4Evah (my total opposite, Dancin4Evah had been created to let me investigate Virtual River Heights without obviously looking like myself); this time we were investigating. I realized after we finished at Shannon's last night (the conversation with the girls and their parents took over an hour, and resulted in lots of tears and grounding) that, although I'd gotten several messages from UrNewReality, I'd never actually come across the avatar in the game. I didn't even know if UrNew-Reality was male or female.

"How do we do this?" Bess asked, sipping from an iced latte she'd brought along.

George turned to her and rolled her eyes. "First," she said, grabbing the coffee from Bess's hand, "we put the beverage far away from the computer equipment. Remember?"

Bess sighed. "You're such a *stickler*."

George shook her head. "I am a person who respects electronics." She placed Bess's latte on a bookshelf sufficiently far away from the computer, then settled back in front of the keyboard. "I think we have to hack into UrNewReality's account. If we use VirtualNancy, we can only look him up if he's had some interaction with you." She glanced at me.

"Not that I know of," I said with a shrug. "Unless I passed her or him in a crowd somewhere."

"That wouldn't matter," George reminded me. "You'd have to actually exchange words with the avatar to look them up."

"Right." I sighed. I'd spent weeks on this game, and it still confused the heck out of me. "So we hack into his account. How do we do that?"

George paused, glancing at Bess and me with a slightly guilty look. "Look, I know how to do it but you have to promise you won't try it yourself," she insisted.

"I promise," I replied quickly.

Bess's lips curled up. "Me too."

George turned back to the computer. "Ok then,'" she replied, going quickly to a search engine where she typed in something that looked like total nonsense to me.

"What are you—?" I asked, but before I could get the question out, the engine returned one result and George clicked on it.

George clicked on a button marked DOWNLOAD ME FREE! and a window came up showing that the program was quickly downloading to my machine.

"What are you putting on my computer?" I asked.

George looked slightly ashamed. "Don't worry, I'll delete it when I'm done," she replied.

I frowned. "George?"

George sighed. "*I* only use it for good," she claimed. "You know that, Nance."

I shook my head. An icon for the program appeared on my desktop, and George clicked it and soon had the application up and running. "I'm going to pretend I never saw any of this," I said. "Your knowledge of computers is so wide and vast, there's no way I could ever understand how you do what you do."

Bess glanced over at me and winked. "Me either."

George just sighed and shook her head. "Whatever." She entered the URL for BetterLife, then typed *UrNewReality* into the Username box. When she clicked in the Password box, she executed some complicated keyboard command that I didn't fully pick up on.

"How are you getting around BetterLife's security features?" Bess asked. "Shouldn't it time you out or something?"

George shrugged. "Well, their security isn't

great to begin with," she said, "so it's not too difficult to override."

I watched the screen. It was almost mesmerizing: the home page kept loading and reloading faster than I could keep track.

Suddenly it stopped. That is, the reloading stopped. I glanced at George, who beamed. Sure enough, when I'd turned back to the screen, the home page was replaced by the bright blue sky and perfectly manicured lawns of Virtual River Heights!

"We're in!" shrieked Bess. "Wow, this is so exciting!"

Slowly the picture shown on my monitor scaled back, and we could see the frame of a window looking out onto a Virtual River Heights street. As the picture pulled back farther, we could see that the window was dirty and cracked, and a few cobwebs showed at the top.

"Yuck," I muttered. "Someone needs to use a little Windex."

George frowned, leaning forward and entering a series of keyboard commands. "It's in View mode," she murmured. "So we're seeing what UrNewReality is seeing, instead of seeing the avatar itself."

"George, look," Bess piped up with a frown of her own. She gestured toward UrNewReality's "stats" that displayed at the bottom of the screen: HUNGER LEVEL. FRIENDS. JOB. STYLE LEVEL. HAPPINESS. Oddly enough, most were set at zero—except the cash meter, which was set at $500, the amount new players were given when they created a new BetterLife character.

"That's weird," I said, leaning forward to get a better look. "It's like they're just starting the game. But it's been over a week since I got my first message from UrNewReality!"

The screen reloaded and we all gasped.

In a dingy, neglected room, covered with cobwebs and dust, a thin, elderly man laid in a small twin bed. The avatar was awake—his eyes stared creepily at a point on the wall—but it was clear that he hadn't moved in years, if ever. Cobwebs covered his body, but you could still see that the man was painfully thin, almost skeletal. Gray hair cascaded down his chin and off of his head like he was Rip van Winkle.

"Creepy," Bess breathed. "Ohhh, this is very, very creepy. Log out!"

I shook my head. "Wait," I said. A window popped up in the middle of the screen.

"That's the first thing they ask you when you create an avatar," I explained. "I remember from when we created VirtualNancy. The first thing you do, the minute the game starts, is try to find a job."

"I remember," Bess breathed. "Oh, remember when VirtualNancy wore that awful sweater and lived in that dingy apartment? You really have to rough it the first few days in this game."

The sweater Bess was referring to had been modeled on an actual sweater I wore quite often in real life, but I decided not to press the issue. "So that means . . ." I began.

". . . he's never been played," George finished, turning to me with a puzzled look.

Bess furrowed her brows. "Someone set up this avatar and then never played him?" she asked. "Why?"

George shrugged. "Maybe they just wanted to use him to send messages," she replied. "The game wasn't as important as having an easy, anonymous way to threaten people. But . . ."

"Doesn't that break a lot of the rules of the

game?" I asked. "First of all, you're not allowed to contact characters you haven't met. Second—"

"—the avatar should be dead," George finished, turning back to the computer with a confused expression. "You have to take *care* of your avatar; that's the whole point of the game. If you stopped taking care of VirtualNancy, she'd eventually run out of food and the character would die."

I nodded. The old man avatar was still lying stock-still on the bed, staring blindly at a spot on the wall. Something about this really gave me the creeps. I shivered.

"Look," said Bess, pointing to a corner of the screen just under UrNewReality's stats. "Isn't there usually a Contact Me button there?"

George frowned. "I *think* so," she replied. "You click on it and it shows you their e-mail address."

"That's right," I agreed. "I think I've used that to contact people in the game privately, when I didn't have their e-mail handy."

Bess turned to George, looking perplexed. "So how are they doing this?" she asked. "I mean, they're breaking some pretty basic rules of the game, right?"

"Right," George agreed, staring at the screen with a sigh. "I mean, the only answer is that

UrNewReality is a hacker. But not even a normal hacker. You would have to know a *lot* about how BetterLife was programmed to figure out how to get around all those rules."

There was a *beep* as another window popped up, and all three of us jumped. But it was just the same window asking UrNewReality if he wanted to look for a job.

"I think it's too late for that," Bess murmured, glancing at the motionless avatar with a shudder.

I leaned forward, grabbing the mouse from George. "Let's let this guy rest," I suggested, clicking the Logout button. "And I'll log on and make sure Dancin4Evah never met this guy. Because isn't that also one of the rules? How is UrNewReality getting in touch with all these people if he doesn't play the game?"

George nodded slowly as the Login screen came up, and I typed in Dancin4Evah's username and password. "You're only supposed to be able to contact people you've met," she agreed. "It's one of their very few security features."

"And actually," Bess added, twisting her mouth into a suspicious smirk, "how is UrNewReality even *finding* these people? How did he know Shannon was back online? How did he know Blondie86 was her?"

I nodded. "He's getting personal information on other players that he shouldn't have access to," I agreed. Just then, Dancin4Evah came onscreen, talking to friends at a virtual club called Lime. He seemed to be perfectly healthy, and with no messages.

George leaned in and did a search for UrNew-Reality, but all we got back was a negative message: DANCIN4EVAH HAS NOT INTERACTED WITH AN AVATAR NAMED URNEWREALITY.

"It looks like no one's caught on that this trendy club kid is really you, Nance," George observed.

"Yeah," I agreed with a sigh. "Well, except Guitarlvr15. He certainly found me easily enough."

George nodded and leaned in, logging Dancin-4Evah out and going back to the login screen. "Nancy, Bess and I have a surprise for you," she announced.

I gave her a confused look—what could it possibly be? But she was looking at Bess, who was beaming.

"We stayed up late last night," Bess explained, "to reunite you with an old friend." She typed VirtualNancy into the Username box, then typed in the password Backfromthedead.

Soon my old avatar appeared onscreen, shelving books in her old job as a bookstore manager at the Virtual River Heights Mall. I quickly checked her stats: All looked to be in order. No new messages, which was a relief. She seemed happy, too—humming to herself as she put the books away. That made me smile.

"Oh my gosh!" I cried, leaning in to get a better look. "She looks just like she did before the—you know . . ."

"Her untimely demise?" George asked.

During the worst of my cyberharassment days, VirtualNancy had been virtually murdered.

"Yeah." I looked at my old avatar wonderingly. "Wow, I missed her. How did you get her back just like she was?"

George smiled. "It took a few hours and a little cheating," she replied, "but new VirtualNancy is just as good as the old one."

I grinned at my friends. "Wow, guys. Thank you. It feels good to know you even have VirtualNancy's back."

I pulled back my chair to let George take over as she clicked a few buttons and checked up on VirtualNancy and UrNewReality's history.

"Nothing," she confirmed, as the screen told us VIRTUALNANCY HAS NOT INTERACTED WITH AN AVATAR NAMED URNEWREALITY.

"Great," I said with a sigh. We were no closer to figuring out who UrNewReality really was. "Now what?"

Bess leaned in. "Well, she has to finish her shift. Then they're showing *The Princess Bride* in the virtual food court. . . ."

George rolled her eyes. "I think Nancy meant, what should we investigate now?"

Just then, a *beep*, and a window popped up announcing YOU HAVE 1 NEW MESSAGE.

"Well," I said, "maybe this will give us a clue." George quickly clicked on Messages, and we all exchanged concerned glances when we saw the sender and subject line: Guitarlvr15, and MYOB.

George opened the message.

SINCE YOU CAN'T MYOB, YOU MIGHT WANT TO CHECK OUT WHAT'S GOING ON AT THE FOOD COURT.

I groaned.

"It could be anything," Bess suggested, trying to sound encouraging. "Maybe they're giving away free burritos!"

"Maybe they're giving away my father's confidential secrets," I countered. George gave me a sympathetic look as she guided VirtualNancy out of the bookstore and toward the food court. "I guess Guitarlvr15 isn't totally down for the count. Maybe UrNewReality wants to ruin my life, but Guitarlvr15 just wants to ruin my father's?"

The virtual food court was crowded with avatars. In the middle of the various levels of seating, a movie screen had been set up.

"The movie starts in a couple minutes," Bess explained.

I had a sinking feeling I knew what was *really* going to start.

In a few seconds, a bright light shone from the rear of the food court, and the movie screen suddenly came to life. It took the crowd a few seconds to realize that they weren't staring at the credits to *The Princess Bride*, however. They were staring at huge projections of my father's confidential files.

"I can't believe they really did this," I muttered.

"Me neither," agreed George, shaking her head. "I realize this means nothing to you, but whoever's behind this is a major hacker. To overwrite the code for the movie screen like that . . ."

The crowd of avatars murmured to each other and moved closer to get a better look. Soon the noise got louder, as everyone turned to his or her friends to talk about what the strange papers might be.

Even the avatar standing next to VirtualNancy seemed fascinated. She nudged VirtualNancy in the arm and then spoke.

KARMAGIRL%!: THEY'RE LEGAL FILES.
VIRTUALNANCY: WHAT?
KARMAGIRL%!: SEE, THEY SAY LEVITT, SOLARI & DREW ON THE TOP. THAT'S A LAW FIRM IN TOWN! YOU KNOW, IN REAL RIVER HEIGHTS.
VIRTUALNANCY: DO YOU KNOW IT?
KARMAGIRL%!: NO, BUT I THINK A GIRL IN MY CLASS, HER FATHER WORKED FOR THEM. I DUNNO WHY THEY WOULD LET THEIR FILES OUT LIKE THIS. I DON'T THINK WE'RE SUPPOSED TO SEE—

Not wanting to hear or see any more, I clicked the button to log VirtualNancy out. "Well, that's it," I said with a sigh. "My father's legal files have gone public. Thank goodness they don't pertain to his case, but . . ."

George and Bess shot me sympathetic looks as my cell phone began to ring.

I picked it up. "It's Ned," I told my friends, glancing at the caller ID. "He was probably playing BetterLife and saw what just happened."

But when I opened the phone and clicked Talk, I wasn't prepared for what I heard.

"Hello? Ned?"

"Nancy?" Ned's voice sounded rattled—totally unlike the calm, cool, collected guy I know. "I'm sorry to bug you when Bess and George are there. But I just got the strangest e-mail. . . ."

THE MOLE

George, Bess and I surrounded Ned as he
sat as his computer.

"So what's this e-mail?" I asked. "Was
it threatening? Did it include any personal information?"

Ned looked perplexed. "Well . . . kind of." He
opened his Internet browser, then typed in the
URL for BetterLife. "And I should have been
more clear before. It's a message I got through
BetterLife, not an e-mail."

The familiar Login screen popped up, and I
watched as Ned typed in his avatar—NattyNed-
145—and his password, which I politely declined
to memorize. Within a few seconds, Ned's avatar

popped up on the Virtual River Heights University campus. I smiled to see Ned's familiar face and lanky body translated into a computer image. He looked different, of course—being two-dimensional can change a person—but somehow, with his khaki pants, striped button-down, and blue pullover sweater, there was no doubt that NattyNed145 was my boyfriend.

He used the mouse to click on his messages, then scanned his in-box. My insides froze when I spotted a familiar name in the Sender box.

UrNewReality.

Was *everyone* I knew going to be a victim of UNR's harassing e-mails?

"It's not so much threatening as . . . odd," Ned explained, highlighting UrNewReality's message and double-clicking to open it up. "I just don't understand. George, I think I have a lot of questions for you." He glanced at George, who just nodded and smiled.

Ned's e-mail popped up to fill the screen. We all leaned in to read:

FROM: URNEWREALITY
TO: NATTYNED145
UNR KNOWS ALL ABOUT U. UNR THINKS U SHOULD CHECK
OUT THE ATTACHMENT. UNR NEEDS A FAVOR. . . . IF U

DON'T WANT EVERY1 TO KNOW ABOUT THE ATTACHED . . .
U WILL BE READY TO HELP WHEN UNR SENDS DETAILS. . . .

I frowned. *If u don't want every1 to know about the attached . . .* This was a blackmail message. Just like the message Shannon had received. UrNewReality was trying to control the people who knew me, trying to get them to—what? What could UrNewReality believe my boyfriend would do to me?

Then it hit me. "What was attached?" I asked. Ned is the most stand-up guy I know, but I still cringed wondering what UrNewReality might think was embarrassing enough to blackmail him with.

Ned shook his head in a *this is ridiculous* gesture as he clicked to open the attachment. I leaned in to get a better look at the screen, sucking in my breath. What could it be?

It was . . .

A *receipt*?

It appeared to be from an online bookstore.

"*The Caucasian Curse*," Bess read out loud, "by Thornton Reading."

"Thornton Reading?" George asked, shooting Ned a disbelieving look. "Is that the crackpot who hosts his own podcast? He sits in his basement and spouts a bunch of racist garbage about minorities taking over the country? *That* guy?"

I frowned. Now the name sounded familiar. I'd read an article about Thornton Reading in one of my father's news magazines, and the guy sounded completely paranoid and horribly prejudiced. I couldn't imagine the Ned I knew having any interest in anything Thornton Reading had written.

Ned sighed. "That's the one," he agreed. "For my social psychology class, I wrote a paper about people's behavior on the Internet—and how the Internet makes it easier for people with radical, angry viewpoints to find like-minded people," he explained. "Thornton Reading's podcast gets thousands of listeners each week, and his website has active message boards with five thousand unique members."

Bess made a face. "That's depressing."

"It is," Ned agreed. "Though it's not clear—are all these people joining because they agree with Thornton Reading? Are they joining out of curiosity? It's hard to tell."

"Ned," I broke in. "Why did you buy the book?"

"For the paper," Ned replied, turning to me. "Come on, Nance. You know I don't share any opinions with this guy. I wanted to see what he had to say firsthand." He wrinkled his nose. "And it was just as bad as you would imagine. I couldn't even finish the book. I threw it away the minute I was done with my paper."

I nodded slowly. I believed him; I had never, in our entire relationship, heard Ned make a prejudiced remark. But that led me to wonder. . . .

"How did UrNewReality get this receipt?" I asked, turning to George.

She frowned, staring at the screen. "It's hard to say for certain," she said finally. "It's related to what I told you earlier—each computer having a unique IP address, et cetera, et cetera." She paused. "Somehow—and I don't know how—it seems that UrNewReality is using BetterLife to get access to the computers of certain players. From there, he—or she—accesses personal files, e-mails, or Internet histories." She looked at Ned. "In this case, he or she probably browsed your e-mails or Internet history to find this purchase." She gestured to the receipt onscreen. "It seems salacious, like something that might embarrass you if people found out about it. So UrNewReality decided to try to use it to blackmail you."

Bess crossed her arms, looking confused. "But

George," she said, "doesn't that mean that everyone who plays BetterLife is at risk of getting hacked? Isn't the game supposed to protect its users' personal information?"

George nodded. "They're *supposed* to," she affirmed. "But clearly we're dealing with a very sophisticated hacker here. He or she knows a lot about BetterLife, and is manipulating the game to his advantage." She furrowed her brows. "Actually," she went on, "someone should alert the owners. . . ."

"There's something else," Ned went on, looking at me with concern. "Everyone who's been hacked—Nancy, Rebecca, Shannon, me—we all have one thing in common."

I swallowed. "Me," I said.

Ned nodded. "And when UrNewReality tried to blackmail Shannon, it was to do something that he or she thought would destroy you, Nancy."

Bess and George looked at me, concern shining in their eyes now. "It's like somebody," George began, "is hacking into people's Internet records to create this army. An army of people who will carry out plots against Nancy."

Yikes. "I don't know if it's that bad yet," I insisted. "I mean, so far, it's just one plot. . . ."

"*So far,*" Ned agreed, frowning. "But that's

because it's just getting started. If I go along with this, Nance, I guarantee they will want me to do something related to you."

Just then, the front door opened, ushering in the sounds of restless footsteps and bookbags being dropped in the hallway.

"And then she said if we go shopping Saturday she'll show me where she got it," a familiar, female voice was saying. "And *then* . . ."

Ned looked up at me and smiled. "Ibrahim?" he called into the hallway. "Arij?"

Ibrahim and Arij were two of the Nickerson family's four houseguests. They were the children of Professor Al-Fulani, a guest professor specializing in peace studies who was teaching at the university. After a housing mix-up, Ned and his parents had offered to allow the Al-Fulanis to stay with them. Ibrahim and Arij were charming, enthusiastic, curious—and Ibrahim, I was slowly realizing, had a crush on me, which could make things awkward. Still, he'd been a wonderful friend and a huge help in investigating the BetterLife case over the last few weeks.

The footsteps continued to the door of the study, and Arij and Ibrahim soon stood in the doorway. Arij beamed at the sight of us; Ibrahim looked slightly uncomfortable.

"Nancy!" Arij greeted me. "Bess! George! And Ned! What are you all doing here?"

"I wanted them to come look at something on the computer," Ned replied with a shrug. "Darn thing confuses me sometimes. Did you have a good day at school?"

"The *best*!" Arij enthused, her dark eyes widening to the size of walnuts. "Today—in history? We watched a movie about the 1960s. And I was so excited by the fashions! Nancy, do you know what it means to dress 'mod'?"

I smiled. "Um, maybe you'd better ask Bess," I replied honestly.

Bess chuckled. "*I* know all about mod fashion," she replied, smiling at Arij. "It's coming back in style, you know! If you're free this weekend, I can take you to some stores that carry some mod looks."

Arij made a little jump of excitement. "Yes! I would love that."

Bess laughed. "All right, it's a date, then."

I looked over at Ibrahim, who seemed to have found something fascinating on the toe of his shoe. "Ibrahim?" I asked. "How was *your* day at school?"

He sighed, nervously scratching his ear, not quite meeting my eye. "It was fine," he told his shoe, "but I have lots of homework. Excuse me."

And then he disappeared from the doorway, never once looking directly at me.

"I should go too," said Arij. "I'm supposed to IM Megan in five minutes. See you later!"

"Bye," I called, and George and Bess and Ned echoed me with their own good-byes. When the teens had left, the four of us met eyes again.

"Ibrahim seemed a little funny to you there," George said, gesturing at me. "You two were such fast friends."

I blushed. I had relied on Ibrahim's help a lot in my early investigations—before I realized that his friendliness was rooted in a little crush. "Maybe he feels a little funny being around Ned and me," I said with a shrug. "It's okay. He needs some time to feel normal around me again."

Ned nodded. "In the meantime," he said, reaching for the mouse, "I'm going to tell UrNew-Reality to go suck an egg."

"No!" I gasped, reaching out to stop him, and to my surprise, Bess and George did exactly the same thing.

"Why?" Ned asked, turning to the three of us with a bemused expression. "I'm not worried about anyone finding out I bought that book. People on campus know me; they know I'm not interested in the ramblings of a racist crackpot. I'm not going to allow some stranger to blackmail me."

I glanced at my friends. I could see they felt the same way I did: Ned was right, but we were getting so close to the mysterious UrNewReality.

"Ned," I said, "I know and you know that that receipt is meaningless. But, if you played along . . ."

Ned sighed. "Played along, Nancy!"

"Just listen. If you played along and found out what UrNewReality wants you to do—maybe we could *finally* get a clue who he is!"

"Or *she*," George reminded me. "Girls can be hackers too."

"Or she," I agreed. "Ned, really—if you're worried about my safety, doesn't it make more sense to play along and find out what this person is really up to? If you tell UrNewReality to go suck an egg, then maybe he or she will give whatever task they have for you to someone else—someone who'll actually go through with it."

That stopped Ned short. He froze at the computer, dropping the mouse, as he appeared to think this over. "Well," he said.

George stepped forward and touched his arm.

"You can be our mole!" she said excitedly. "You can be working for us on the inside. See what they want you to do, but tell us everything."

Ned looked at me. He didn't look thrilled about this; in fact, his expression told me that he was distinctly uncomfortable. But he was concerned enough for my safety that he was willing to go along with it.

"Please, Ned," I urged, leaning over to rest my hand on his shoulder. "We *have* to figure out who this person is. If not, who knows how long he can harass me by computer?"

Ned seemed to think this over, then he looked up at me and sighed. "Okay," he agreed. "But I hope it goes without saying, I'm not carrying out any of UrNewReality's little missions! I'll see what he or she has to say, but that's it. It ends there."

I gave him a big hug. "Of course, Ned." I smiled. "Just the information you get is enough for me."

When I turned around, though, I could see George was still frowning. "We should contact the owners of BetterLife," she murmured, gesturing at the computer screen. "Those men you saw speak at the university. What were their names?"

I made a face. "Robert Sung and Jack Crilley."

The memory of meeting them was not a pleasant one. They hadn't reacted very well to the questions I'd asked them, or the implication that their game had security failures that made it easy for users to lie about their true identities.

"Excuse me, Ned," George said, gently nudging Ned away from the computer. She sat down and started clicking on different BetterLife screens, trying to locate a contact number, I guess. When that didn't work, she went to a search engine and typed in *BetterLife contact number*, but none of the results it returned seemed to contain a phone number. In fact, oddly enough, there seemed to be very little information available about how to contact anyone with a BetterLife problem.

Sighing, George typed in the BetterLife URL again. "There's a FAQ and a message board," she complained. "And it looks like there's one general e-mail for *all* BetterLife-related questions and comments. Who knows how often they check that?"

Bess shrugged. "It looks like our only choice, though," she said. "Right?"

George shook her head. "Right," she agreed reluctantly. I watched as she clicked on the E-MAIL US! button and began typing up a quick but urgent message about a hacker using the program to steal users' private information. She left her e-mail, and home and cell numbers as contact info. She signed the e-mail "Looking forward to hearing from you very soon, George Fayne."

She clicked Send, pressing down very deliberately on the mouse button. "I guess we've done all we can do for right now," she said.

"Agreed," I replied, and Bess and Ned nodded.

We were all silent for a minute, then Bess piped up. "While we're here," she said slyly, gesturing at the BetterLife screen, "maybe we can quickly take VirtualNancy shopping?"

I groaned.

SURPRISE MEETING

I was awakened from a deep sleep the next morning. I'd been having a dream where I was playing BetterLife as VirtualNancy, but everyone I was interacting with—Ned, Bess, George, even Ibrahim—was their real, three-dimensional self, and I was my VirtualNancy avatar. Then, suddenly, the setting changed and we were in *real* River Heights—not virtual River Heights. But I was still VirtualNancy! I kept trying to shout, to use my voice, but whenever I wanted to communicate, I had to type what I wanted to say into a keyboard and everyone else would read it on their PDAs.

"Oh, Nancy," Ned said sympathetically in my dream, resting a hand on my oddly smooth, oddly glowing arm. "You know why I'm doing this, right? It's for you. . . ."

"Nancy!" A female, somewhat frustrated voice interrupted my dream. I realized that I was in my bed, and someone was shaking my arm—it was our housekeeper and good friend, Hannah Gruen. "Nancy! Can't you hear me? It's for you. The phone is for you."

I blinked awake. "What time is it?" I asked groggily.

"Eight thirty," Hannah replied, taking my hand and slipping our cordless phone into it. "I didn't want to wake you, but George said it was important."

George? I held the phone to my ear. "Hello?"

"Nancy!" George cried. Hannah patted my arm and backed out of my bedroom. I mouthed a silent *thank you* to her, and she smiled and waved.

"Get up and get some clothes on, Nance. You and I have a hot date at the library."

I rubbed my eyes. "Huh?" I asked. "George? Slow down. *What* are we doing at the library?"

George sighed. "Only making the Internet safe for future generations! I was woken up this morning by a phone call from none other than the *public relations representative* for Mr. Robert Sung and Mr. Jack Crilley."

I blinked. The BetterLife creators? "They called you back?" I cried, too surprised to hide the disbelief from my voice.

"They did indeed," George sang, "and thanks for the vote of confidence. Yeah, to be honest, I was surprised too, but this woman said they read my e-mail and were *very* concerned about BetterLife being used to hack into its users' lives."

"Huh," I muttered. When I'd met Jack Crilley and Robert Sung, they hadn't exactly seemed very concerned about their users' privacy or safety.

"It just so happens," George was going on, "that their security consultant, a Ms. Dorothy Bilowski, lives about twenty minutes away. So the PR rep set up a meeting for us today at 10 a.m. at the River Heights library. Be there or be square!"

I shook my head. This was all falling into place, almost too easily. "She just happens to live here?" I asked.

"I know it's weird," George replied, slowing the pace of her words a bit, "but it's not that crazy in the world of computers. If you're an expert in something—say, setting up billing systems, or security features—then you can work as a consultant to lots of different companies. They'll hire you just to set up their system, then you move on. Consultants live all over the country. So it's a coincidence, sure, but definitely possible."

I took a breath, considering all of this. "How are we going to show her what's been going on?" I asked.

"That's the thing," George said. "I've got my work cut out for me, actually. She wants me to track down all the evidence I can and put it on my laptop. We'll bring that to the meeting so she can have a look, and hopefully figure out what's going on."

George went on to ask me for Shannon's phone number, so she could get her password as Blondie86. She'd already called Ned for his.

"Did you know his BetterLife password is blueeyedgirl?" George asked. I could hear the smirk in her voice. And I immediately felt myself blushing.

"That's sweet," I murmured.

George went back to her earlier gruff tone. "Well, get up, Nance," she insisted. "We've got a big day ahead of us. And Bess is working today, so it's just you and me, kid."

"Roger that," I replied.

After saying good-bye, I quickly showered, dressed, and ran downstairs for some oatmeal, courtesy of Hannah. By the time George came to pick me up, I was settled at the kitchen table, reading the paper.

BETTERLIFE SUBSCRIPTION PLAN DEBUTS SATURDAY, a headline in the business section screamed. In smaller letters below, it said: *Co-founders Predicted to Make Millions.* That meant Robert Sung and Jack Crilley. BetterLife was currently and always had been a free program, but it was amazingly popular, and as Shannon Fitzgerald showed, many of its frequent users were like addicts— they depended on their BetterLife life to keep them sane. On Saturday, a new subscription plan would become available that would allow users to pay $19.99 a month in order to become an "enhanced" user. Enhanced users would get various advantages in the game; for example, it would be easier for them to secure high-paying jobs, and their characters would get more information about the other players in the game. But also, enhanced users would be able to further personalize their avatars, uploading their favorite music, using their favorite brands, and even making custom "skins" of actual clothes from their wardrobes for their avatars to wear.

It's unusual for people to pay for something they can get for free, but still, millions of users were expected to sign up for the subscription plan in the first couple weeks. Sung and Crilley were already making money from advertising in the BetterLife world, but now that they'd be making money directly from their players, they would become very rich men.

In a way, I thought, it was particularly impressive that they'd reacted so quickly during this week of all weeks. I supposed it was a good sign that they were so concerned about the security problems, even as they prepared to unleash this new, lucrative service.

"Hey," I greeted George, climbing into the passenger seat of her car. "Did you get everything you needed onto your laptop?"

"Sure did," George replied with a smile. "I can't wait to show it all to Ms. Bilowski. It's nice to think we might be able to nip this whole cyberharassment thing in the bud through technology."

I smiled. *It would be nice*, I thought, *but something tells me it's not going to be that simple.* George pulled back into the street, and we made our way to the library.

"Where is the computer section?" George asked at the front desk of the River Heights library.

That's where our meeting with Dorothy Bilowski was supposed to take place.

"You don't know?" I asked George, nudging her teasingly. "You're such a computer buff, I would think you'd have a trail worn into the carpet."

George made a face. "It's all computer manuals, Nance," she replied. "Novice stuff. When I need a copy of *Windows XP for Dummies*, maybe I'll pay it a visit."

The volunteer at the front desk was looking from me to her with an amused expression. "It's in the basement," she told George. "Straight behind you, first door on your right, down one flight and to the left."

"Thanks," George said with a smile. We turned around and made our way downstairs.

"I don't think I've spent much time in the library basement," I murmured, lowering my voice when I heard how it echoed in the stairway.

"Me neither," George replied softly, matching my tone. "It's so quiet down here on a weekday morning! It's kind of creeping me out."

The basement level of the library was quiet, and a little dark, lit by small windows at the very tops of the walls. Every section we passed was completely empty. I wondered if George and I were the only people down there.

"Here we go," George said, gesturing to a rectangular wooden table in front of a few shelves' worth of old computer manuals. "I think this is where Ms. Bilowski wanted to meet. I guess we can just settle down here."

We each pulled out a chair and made ourselves comfortable at the table. It was overwhelmingly quiet, and for a few minutes we just sat there, silent and awkward.

"What time is it?" I whispered finally.

George held up her watch. It was 10:06.

"She may have had trouble finding the library," George whispered with a shrug.

I shrugged back. "I'm not worried," I replied. "I'm sure she'll show up."

We lapsed back into silence.

And I *was* sure she'd show up. Sure when I asked George for the time again at 10:09, and again at 10:13. At 10:18, though, I was starting to have my doubts.

I glanced pointedly at George's PDA, which she'd placed on the table next to her laptop. "Did you give her your cell phone number?" I asked.

"Of course I did," George replied, picking up the PDA to examine it. "It's on silent mode. And

I don't get great reception down here. But it looks like she hasn't called."

I sighed. On the PDA, I saw the clock tick to 10:19.

"Maybe you should go upstairs and check it where you have better reception?" I asked. "I mean, it's not like—"

But I never got to finish. Right at that moment, the near-silence was cut by a terrified female scream. *"Aaaauuuuuuugh!"*

And there was a *clunk*, like something falling.

George and I exchanged a glance. Neither one of us said anything, but we both sprang up from our seats and darted toward the source of the scream. It seemed to be coming from a section of books three rows down and two aisles over. As we got closer, I heard moaning. And soon we came upon a blond girl—she couldn't have been more than fifteen—sprawled out on the library floor. Above her, a rolling ladder loomed malevolently.

"Ohhhh," she moaned, clutching her ankle. "Oh, ouch . . . I can't believe I did that. . . ."

"Are you okay?" George asked, kneeling by her side. "Did you fall?"

The girl moaned again. "Ohhh . . . yeah." She glanced up at George gratefully. "I must have been up near the top, and my foot just totally missed the next rung. The next thing I knew . . ." She gestured around her, at the floor.

"Are you hurt?" I asked, kneeling on her other side. "Can you move your arms and legs okay? Is anything broken?"

The girl looked up at me, then bit her lip, as if considering. "My ankle hurts a lot," she replied.

"Which one?" I asked. "This one?" I touched her left ankle, but got no response. I touched her right, too, but still the girl made no outward signs that she was in pain. A few seconds after I touched her right ankle, she said clearly, "Yeah—that one." But it was long enough after I'd been squeezing her ankle, that it seemed odd to me that she didn't make a peep until then.

"Can you move it?" asked George. She didn't seem to notice the girl's hesitation.

The girl bit her lip again. "Um . . . yeah," she replied, rotating the ankle in what seemed like a lot of movement for an injured person. "I think it might be sprained, though. It hurts *so* much. . . ."

George looked sympathetically at the girl, then down at me, by her feet. "Maybe we'd better take you to the emergency room," she suggested. "If it hurts that much, you should really get an X-ray."

The girl swallowed and sat up a little bit.

"Noooo," she insisted. "Don't be silly. I'm sure it's fine."

I tried to catch her eye, but she was looking down now. "You were just saying you were in a lot of pain," I reminded her. "It's really better to be safe than sorry."

"Oh, no," the girl insisted, looking up and shooting me a forced smile. "It actually—it feels a lot better now. Look, I think I can even stand on it."

Oddly quickly for someone who had just fallen from a good height, the girl pulled her legs under her and slowly stood. She made a big show of testing her weight on the "bad" leg, then smiled. "It feels fine now," she insisted. "Good as new. Thanks for your help, but I should get going. . . ." She began backing away in the opposite direction from where George and I had come.

"Wait, are you sure?" George called, taking a few steps after her. "You didn't seem okay a few seconds ago!"

"I'm fine!" the girl cried, waving behind her without turning around. "Thanks for your help!" And she disappeared around a corner, and was gone.

George turned and caught my eye. "That was odd," she murmured.

"Very," I agreed. "But maybe in the time it took to help her, our mystery guest showed up. Come on, let's get back."

We walked slowly back to the computer section. As we reached our aisle and looked toward the table where we'd been sitting, it was clear that no one had come to join us. The section was as silent and deserted as ever. But as we stepped closer, we noticed that *something* had changed . . .

"My laptop!" George cried, breaking into a run. She quickly reached the table, pulling out our chairs, looking all around. But the computer was gone.

Just then, in the silence, I heard footfalls running to our left. I turned around. "George!" I cried.

A figure—just a blur, really, in a trench coat and baseball cap—was running away with George's laptop clutched in his or her hands! As soon as she saw it, George took off at a fast clip toward the figure. I followed, and together, we trailed the trench-coated thief up the stairs and through a side exit.

"Stop him!" George cried, getting closer and closer to the figure. "Thief!"

The security guard at the front desk turned around and looked as though he was deciding whether to believe us, but George and I were already way ahead of him. We darted out of the library and stood on the steps, shielding our eyes from the sun as we searched the street for the mysterious thief.

"There!" George cried, pointing at the sidewalk across the street, where our trench-coated villain was running north, toward downtown River Heights.

Without another word, we both barreled down the steps after the thief, pausing only briefly to look for oncoming cars before we darted across the street. The thief was already a block ahead of us, entering River Heights' congested main thoroughfare where shoppers and late-breakfast-eaters crowded the stores and sidewalk cafes.

"We need to speed up!" George cried between gasps of breath. "He's going to lose us in the crowd!"

I struggled to pick up my pace, my lungs burning as we raced down the next block and into the main drag. George paused for just a second to survey the scene. The thief had run by several clumps of slow-moving pedestrians, and it seemed, for the moment anyway, we'd lost sight of our target.

I skidded to a stop behind George as she frowned, shielding her eyes again to scan the sidewalk. "We have to catch him," she muttered under her breath. "If I lose that laptop, you don't understand, Nancy—my life will be a shambles!"

"What do you *have* on there?" I asked, honestly curious. If someone stole my ancient-but-beloved desktop, I would be sad, but not completely ruined. I'd be out a few e-mails and Internet passwords, sure, but I was pretty sure I'd be able to start over.

"All of my finances," George began listing, "my calendar, my contacts . . . my Christmas card list . . . my goals for the week and month . . . every e-mail, letter, or paper I've ever written . . ." Suddenly her eyes lit up. "There!" she cried, pointing to our local pharmacy. Sure enough, our thief was just darting through the automatic front doors.

We ran after him, pausing briefly to cross the street. By the time we ran headlong into the store—startling a few elderly customers who stood up front, waiting to pay—our thief was nowhere to be seen.

"He has to be in here," I said, stating the obvious. "There's only the one door."

George nodded grimly. "You run to the back," she instructed, "and I'll stay up front. We'll search every aisle. When you find him, yell!"

I did as George instructed, running to the back

of the store, where the pharmacist shot me an annoyed look. She probably thought we were a couple of bored teenagers playing chase in their nice quiet store, so I decided not to take offense. Moving quickly, I scanned every aisle, but I saw nothing—nothing, that is, that resembled a trench-coated mystery man holding a stolen laptop. I did see lots of confused elderly people. (Mental note: It seems the elderly really like to pick up their pills on weekday mornings.)

Suddenly the soft Muzak playing over the store's sound system was cut by a loud, crazy "HAAAAH!" that I instantly recognized as George. "NANCY! AISLE NINE!" she shouted. I then heard rapid, thumping footfalls as George (I presumed) barreled after our mystery thief (I presumed). By the time I got my wits about me and started charging to aisle nine, George shrieked.

"*Nancy!* Front of the store! He's getting away!"

Changing course as fast as I could, I dodged a frightened-looking lady holding a gray-haired wiener dog and charged to the front of the store. There, I saw our mystery man (closer now, I could see it was a male) emerge from an aisle to my left. Darting forward with all the strength I had, I somehow managed to get ahead of him, cutting him off from the front door and forcing him back toward the aisle. Just then, an almost-out-of-breath George came charging out of the aisle he came from. Our thief hesitated for a second, then ran down an aisle on the far right side of the store.

George looked at me wearily. "Me," she said simply, gesturing to the aisle behind her. "You," she went on, pointing down the aisle where the thief had disappeared. "We . . ." She gestured to imply that we would both run down the aisles, meeting at the back of the store—and trapping the thief.

I nodded. "Gotcha." And just like that, we both ran off to trap the thief.

The aisle he had run down was the cosmetics and perfume aisle, and I spotted our thief trying to hide behind a display for some young pop star's (I'm sure Bess would be able to identify her) new signature scent. This close, I could see more clearly that he had disguised himself with a trench coat, a baseball cap pulled low over his eyes, dark sunglasses, and a muffler knotted high across his jaw. He was only feet away, and yet I still couldn't see any of his identifying features. When he spotted me, he turned and tried to run to the back of the store, but George was already jogging up the aisle from that direction. "Freeze!" she shouted at him.

Desperate, the thief picked up the tester from the perfume display and brandished it at us like a weapon. "Stop!" he said in a muffled voice.

George sighed. "I'm sure that smells terrible," she said, "but still, you have got to be kidding me." She held out her hand. "My laptop, please."

Defeated, the thief put the perfume back on the display and handed over the laptop. "I'm sorry," he said in the same muffled voice.

George accepted her laptop and glanced at the thief warily, settling down cross-legged on the pharmacy's floor. "Stay right there," she instructed the thief as she powered up her computer. He stood, clearly uncomfortable, fiddling with the gloves he wore. After a moment, a chime implied that the computer was powering up, and George frowned as she scanned the desktop and clicked on a few files. After a minute or two, she closed the laptop and turned back to our thief.

"Okay," she said. "Everything appears to be in order. Now, do you want to tell me just what the heck you think you were doing?"

The thief didn't say anything. Even though I couldn't see his expression, his body language was pure deer-in-the-headlights. After a few seconds, he shook his head.

"All right," I said, growing weary of the game.

"Come on. Let's see who you are." I reached over to grab his cap and sunglasses. He shifted away, but I was too fast; I grabbed the brim of his hat and then knocked the sunglasses off his face. "Voila!" I shouted, gesturing toward George. "Our—"

But before I could say "thief," I caught sight of our culprit and was too stunned to continue. I gasped, and heard George do the same.

Our thief looked miserable, like he would have done anything to get out of there. After a moment, I got my breath back and turned to George.

She was clearly just as surprised as I was.

"Ibrahim!"

CYBER SETUP

"**I**'m so sorry," Ibrahim gushed, shaking his head and sitting down on the low shelf of the perfume display. "I'm so sorry. But I don't understand, Nancy! I don't understand what you want from me."

"Ibrahim?" I asked, not understanding. He had his head in his hands now, and was clearly very upset. I could see tears forming at the corners of his eyes. But I had no idea what he was talking about. "What do you mean, what I want from you?"

Ibrahim shook his head and wiped at his eyes. "I should not have sent the e-mail," he went on. "I'm sorry I tried to be your friend, Nancy! I know, you are with Ned. But why can't you just let me be?"

I glanced at George, who looked just as lost as I felt. "E-mail?" she asked.

"What e-mail?" I added, turning to Ibrahim. "Ibrahim, I'm so sorry you're upset. But I honestly have no idea what you're talking about, or what this has to do with your stealing George's laptop."

Ibrahim looked up at me as sharply as if I had slapped him. "I did not *steal* George's laptop," he replied. "I did exactly what you told me to do."

Okay, now it was like he was speaking Martian. I looked to George for an explanation. "I . . ." I began, but couldn't figure out how to continue.

George shook her head. "Listen," she said, placing her hand on Ibrahim's shoulder. "Let's start at the beginning. You sent an e-mail?"

Ibrahim blushed and nodded, looking at me ruefully. "Nancy knows all about it," he insisted.

"I don't," I replied. "Ibrahim, listen, I can see that you're very upset, but I truly don't know what you're talking about. Will you explain it to me?"

Ibrahim's eyes took on a glimmer of uncertainty as George patted his shoulder. "What was the e-mail about?" she asked gently.

Ibrahim sighed. He rubbed his eyes, then his temples as he cast his eyes to the floor. "It was an e-mail from me to Nancy," he began. "It was . . . it was . . . oh, it would be better to show you." He gestured toward George's laptop, and she handed it to him. He opened the top, bringing it back to life, and brought up the Internet browser. After logging in to his e-mail and clicking on a few links, Ibrahim wordlessly handed George the computer back. He looked back at the floor as I stepped behind George to see the screen. He had brought up an e-mail from his "sent messages" folder.

FROM: IBRAHERO@RHHS.EDU
TO: SLEUTHGAL18@FASTMAIL.COM
NANCY,
I WAS THINKING ABOUT YOU TODAY AND SMILING. I AM
SO HAPPY TO HAVE MET YOU AND BEEN ABLE TO SPEND
TIME WITH YOU THESE PAST FEW WEEKS. YOU ARE SO
SMART AND GENEROUS, AND I THINK YOUR RED HAIR
IS VERY PRETTY. I WISH WE COULD SPEND MORE TIME
TOGETHER. I KNOW THAT YOU ARE DATING NED, WHO IS A
VERY FINE PERSON, BUT I WANTED YOU TO KNOW I THINK
YOU ARE WONDERFUL. MAYBE IN THE FUTURE WE WILL
MEET AGAIN.
WITH LOVE,
IBRAHIM

I felt myself blushing, reading over George's shoulder. Okay—it wasn't exactly a declaration of love. But I cringed thinking of how hard it must have been for Ibrahim to send, and how awful it must be to see me read it for the first time under these circumstances.

"Thank you," I said softly, reaching over to touch Ibrahim's shoulder.

He just grunted in response, not looking up from the floor.

George shot me an uncomfortable look that told me she felt as bad as I did. "Okay," she went on in her gentle voice. "So you sent this e-mail. What makes you think—"

"Wait!" I interrupted as I realized: "I never got it."

George raised an eyebrow. "You didn't?" she asked. Placing the laptop on a high shelf, she began typing an address in the web browser. "Are you sure? You've checked your e-mail recently?"

"Just this morning," I affirmed. I'd done a quick check before jumping in the shower. "That message wasn't there. In fact, there wasn't anything except spam."

George frowned. "Huh."

Ibrahim looked up at me curiously. "You . . . you never got the e-mail?" he asked.

"No," I confirmed.

His expression lightened a bit. But he still looked puzzled. "Then that means . . ." He frowned. "I don't understand."

George touched his shoulder again. "What's up, Ibrahim?" she asked him. "I still don't understand how that e-mail led to you taking this laptop. What's the connection?"

Ibrahim glanced at me, then back at George. He looked like a little lost boy—like something in his mind just wasn't making sense. "I . . . got this message," he said slowly, as though he were trying to figure it out as he spoke. "On BetterLife."

George met my eye immediately. *A message. On BetterLife.* Just like Shannon, who'd been blackmailed into stealing my father's files . . . and Ned, who UrNewReality was *trying* to blackmail into who knows what?

"Can we see it, Ibrahim?" I asked quietly. "Can you bring it up on George's laptop?"

Ibrahim glanced up at me and nodded. "Sure," he agreed. I was relieved to see that he appeared less angry with me. I guess once he realized I never saw his e-mail, I suddenly became a lot less threatening.

George handed the computer over, and Ibrahim logged on to BetterLife. Quickly accessing his messages, he selected one and immediately handed the computer back to George, almost as though he didn't want to be exposed to the message again. "There," he said, looking hesitantly over at me again. "Truly, Nancy, you had nothing to do with this?"

I shrugged. "Ibrahim, I haven't sent you a message on BetterLife in weeks."

"Oh boy," George said, shaking her head as she read Ibrahim's suspicious message. "Looks like our old friend UrNewReality, Nan."

I stepped up behind her, peering over her shoulder at the message.

UNR KNOWS U. UNR KNOWS U R IN OVER UR HEAD HERE. UNR NEEDS A FAVOR, AND UNLESS U WANT EVERY1 2 KNOW ABOUT UR CRUSH, U WILL DO WHAT UNR SAYS.

The e-mail Ibrahim had sent to me was copied in at the bottom.

"Wow," I breathed. "This person—whoever UrNewReality is—is reaching out to practically everyone I know!"

Ibrahim looked uncomfortable. I turned to face him, suddenly realizing what he must have thought.

"You thought this was how I'd respond to your e-mail?" I asked him. "That I'd read it and immediately tried to turn around and use it against you?"

Ibrahim looked sheepish. "When you put it like that, it seems unlikely," he admitted, shrugging his shoulders. "But at the time . . . I didn't see who else it could be. You were the only one I sent the e-mail to, Nancy. I didn't want to believe it, but I thought maybe I hadn't really known you at all."

I sighed. "Oh, Ibrahim." I leaned closer and tapped him on the shoulder. "For the record," I told him, "*this* is how I would have responded to your e-mail." I opened my arms, he leaned in, and I gave him a big hug. "Thank you," I repeated. "It means a lot that such a nice person thinks so much of me."

Ibrahim gently pulled away, looking a little embarrassed. "Well," he said, looking into his lap and blushing, "thank you."

George made a face. "Enough, enough mushiness!" she insisted. "We have a mystery here, people! Ibrahim, you must have gotten another message with instructions on what to do today. Where is it?"

He took the computer back and selected the

message. "Here it is," he said, handing the computer back.

I leaned over George's shoulder again. The message read:

UNR IS READY FOR YOUR HELP. UNR NEEDS 2 GET BACK
SOMETHING THAT WAS STOLEN AND IS VERY IMPORTANT.
U WILL GO 2 RIVER HEIGHTS PUBLIC LIBRARY AT 10:10
AM. U WILL WAIT IN THE BASEMENT. U WILL WEAR A
DISGUISE. WHEN U HEAR A SHOUT . . . YOU WILL RUN 2
THE COMPUTER SECTION. THERE, U WILL FIND A SILVER
LAPTOP.
TAKE IT.
U WILL RECEIVE ANOTHER MESSAGE WITH INSTRUCTIONS
ON WHERE 2 SEND IT. . . .

George shook her head in amazement. "'Something that was stolen and is very important,'" she read with a sigh. "UrNewReality was probably referring to all the messages from him on my computer, but it reads like the laptop was stolen." She glanced at Ibrahim. "Is that what you thought?"

He nodded, looking ashamed. "I still felt strange taking something that wasn't mine," he explained, "but then I told myself, if something of mine was stolen I would want it back. And I wanted to help Nancy—even though I was angry she was making me do this."

George nodded. "And you didn't see us there."

Ibrahim shook his head. "Not until you started chasing me," he replied. "Then, I felt terrible— like something had to be wrong. If Nancy wanted me to steal back her computer, why would she be chasing me?"

"It wasn't," I said. "It wasn't my computer, and I wasn't the one blackmailing you, Ibrahim. I'm so sorry you got caught up in this. I really never meant for you to get hurt."

Ibrahim looked uncomfortable again, shaking his head and looking down at his shoes. "It's all right, Nancy," he said quietly, almost too quietly to hear. "I am leaving soon with my family, and you are with Ned anyway. . . . I should learn my lesson and stay away."

"Ibrahim," I scolded. "Don't be ridiculous."

But he still looked unconvinced, refusing to meet my eye. Instead, he looked at George. "May I go now?" he asked.

George looked to me, surprised. "I guess so," she replied. "I think we've figured out what really happened here. Just promise us, Ibrahim, if you get any other strange messages, you'll contact us right away."

Ibrahim nodded, meeting my eyes briefly and nodding. "Good-bye, George. Good-bye, Nancy."

"Bye, Ibrahim," I said softly. Turning toward the front of the store, my friend—who it now seemed wanted to forget I existed—shuffled off.

When I pulled my eyes away from Ibrahim, George was looking at me sympathetically. "Don't worry about it, Nance. He just feels awkward."

"I know," I said. And I did. It just felt strange to upset someone I truly did like, all because he liked me more. I shook my head to clear it and turned to George. "You heard what he said, right?"

George smiled, getting my drift immediately. "About waiting for the shout?"

I nodded. "Seems a little coincidental, huh?"

Without another word, we picked up our things and headed out of the pharmacy, back toward the library. The security guard looked a little surprised to see us again—after we'd last run from the library screaming "thief!"—but seemed to decide to let bygones be bygones.

"Excuse me," I greeted him, sidling up with George at my side. "But has anyone been down to the basement in—oh, say the last twenty minutes?" That was about how long we'd been gone, chasing Ibrahim and then questioning him.

The guard—whose nametag read BILL—shook his head. "The basement? No ma'am, I've been standing here at the only staircase for the last hour. Only people to go up and down are you two, that kid you were chasing earlier, and a young girl—left right before the two of you."

George glanced at me. I could tell she was thinking the same thing I was: The girl must have been the girl we helped once she fell from the ladder. "Did she look hurt in any way?" George asked. "Was she limping?"

Bill shook his head. "No, actually she seemed to be in a hurry," he replied with a shrug. "Ran right out the door like someone was chasing her. A few minutes later, the boy and the two of you came up."

We nodded. "I see. Well, thanks a lot for your help," I said.

I looked at George and nodded toward the stairway.

"She was *running*," George marveled, "and our security consultant never showed up. Isn't that interesting?"

We reached the basement level and made a bee-line for the computer section. Indeed, we seemed to be the only patrons down there now. The table was empty, the chairs still pulled out from where we'd left them. Whoever our "security consultant" was . . . she really had never showed.

"Let's take a quick look at where the girl fell," I suggested. Wasting no time—it felt creepy being in the basement alone—we headed over to the section where the ladder still stood. I climbed up a few steps, and took a look around at the books that surrounded me.

"These are encyclopedias," I said wonderingly, "in *German*, I think." I lifted one of the heavy books from its place on the shelf. Clouds of dust released into the air, tickling my nose and making me cough.

An old bookplate was pasted onto the endpapers:

THESE ENCYCLOPEDIAS DONATED BY HEIDI KRAUS
A PROUD GERMAN CITIZEN AND RESIDENT OF RIVER
HEIGHTS FOR THIRTY YEARS

Well, that explained it. "They were donated," I told George.

George cocked an eyebrow. "It seems awfully unlikely," she said, "that our falling girl—who looked, at most, sixteen years old—was hanging around to check out German encyclopedias."

I nodded grimly. "Between that, and the security consultant never showing up . . . you know what I'm thinking?"

George nodded. "I do, but go ahead."

I frowned, climbing down from the ladder. "This whole thing was a setup."

TEENYBOPPER SQUABBLES

"This isn't right, Nance," George muttered as we walked back to her car. Since we'd left the library, she seemed more and more agitated. "I'm going to try the PR woman again who called me this morning."

So far, George had tried to reach the number that had called her this morning (it was stored in her phone's call log) twice. Both times, the phone had rung and rung, with no answer.

Now, George sighed sharply, implying that she'd reached yet another dead end. "No answer," she confirmed, hitting the End button. "That seems kind of odd for someone in public relations, right? To not answer the phone?"

I nodded. Everyone knew that a PR person's job was to make the company they worked for look good. Avoiding people's calls, and not even having a voicemail box set up, wasn't exactly the best way to do that.

We had reached George's car, and she sighed again, shoving her phone into her pocket in frustration. "This is huge, Nancy," she said again. "We were just set up by the most successful online gaming programmers in the country."

"Either that," I added, "or someone's hacked in to their e-mail system."

George's eyes lit up. "I didn't think of that," she admitted. "But if UrNewReality is able to hack into *our* computers with such ease, why *wouldn't* he or she be able to hack into the company's e-mail?"

I frowned. "One thing's for sure," I said. "Someone at the BetterLife Company should know about this."

George nodded. "And it looks like e-mail's not working," she said grimly. "What are our other options? Is there any other way for us to get in touch directly with Robert Sung or Jack Crilley?"

I cringed, remembering my first meeting with the two programmers who would soon be millionaires. It had gotten pretty tense—tense enough to make their host, a professor from the computer science department named Professor Frank, uncomfortable. Suddenly it came to me.

"That's *it*!" I cried.

George looked skeptical. "What's it?" she asked. "Please Nance—don't tell me you want to write them a letter."

I rolled my eyes. "*No*, George." I shook my head. "I'm not a total technophobe. I just remembered, a computer science professor at the university hosted Sung and Crilley when they came to speak to the student body. He *must* have contact information for them!"

George's skeptical look vanished. "That actually makes a lot of sense." She gave me a goofy grin. "Nancy, I've underestimated you yet again. Shall we head to the university?" She asked.

"We shall," I said with a queenly air as George climbed into the car and unlocked my door. "Let's see if we can arrange a meeting with Professor Frank."

We were lucky; we arrived at the university's computer science center just as Professor Frank was finishing up his office hours. We waited on a bench outside his office while a couple students finished up, then walked in.

"Hello," said the professor, looking at us curiously. "Are you students of mine?"

George shook her head. "We're not," she clarified. "But we live in River Heights, and we just became aware of an issue you—"

"*Wait* a minute," the professor interrupted her, adjusting his eyeglasses and staring at me. "I remember you! You're the young rabble-rouser who attacked Jack and Robert after their lecture."

George shot me a pointed glance. I knew she was reacting to the fact that he'd called them by their first names; clearly they were fairly close.

"I wouldn't call it *attacking*," I said to Professor Frank, defending myself.

He smiled; I could see he was kind of amused. "What would you call it, then?" he asked.

I shrugged, trying to look innocent. "Asking some important questions?" I asked. "Questions that, I might add, they never really answered?"

Professor Frank sat still for a moment, absorbing that, but then chuckled. I'd won him over. "All right, sit down," he invited us, gesturing to the modern plastic chairs that faced his desk. "I don't have a lot of time, but I'm curious to hear what you have to say."

George didn't mince words. "Professor Frank,"

she began as soon as her bottom hit the chair, "we have reason to believe that an employee of BetterLife is hacking the game and using it to collect personal information on its users. Either that, or a very sophisticated hacker has targeted the site."

Professor Frank looked a little surprised by our claims, but he nodded moderately. "What is your evidence?" he asked George. "What leads you to believe this?"

George glanced at me, and I sighed. Where to begin? "It's a lot of things," I replied, trying to collect all of our evidence in my head. "For the last couple weeks," I continued, "I have been cyberharassed, and I believe it's all coming from the game."

Professor Frank nodded, still looking vaguely amused. He clearly wasn't going to accept our story at face value. We would have to prove it to him.

"Define *cyberharassed*," he instructed me. "Some negative comments in the game? A mean e-mail or two?"

I shook my head. "Hardly," I replied. "Actually, someone hacked into my account and made it look like my avatar performed a hate crime against one of my good friends. Then they created an avatar that looked like my boyfriend, to fool me into thinking it was him. They *killed* me in the game. Meanwhile, they used e-mails and the Internet to set up babysitting jobs for me and not tell me about it, order pizzas I didn't want, stuff like that."

Professor Frank nodded warily. "That sounds very annoying," he said.

"Not just *annoying*," George put in, starting to look annoyed herself. "It's cyberharassment. Nancy didn't mention that the reason she's on the game at all, and the reason she came to the lecture that night, is that young girls were using the game to bully each other—making each others' lives pretty much unlivable!"

The professor looked sympathetic, but still he shrugged. "Young girls are often unkind to each other," he said. "It's a difficult age. You can't blame the programmers for kids using the program to do the very same things they're doing in real life. In fact, that's really the point of the game."

George caught my eye. I could see she was fuming. I decided to give it another try.

"The specific reason we're here," I explained, "is that in the last week or so, this cyberharasser—his avatar is UrNewReality—has been targeting people who know me. He—"

"Or she," George inserted.

"Or *she*," I agreed. "He or she uses Better-Life in some way to gain access to their personal e-mails and files. They *then* use something from those personal e-mails and files to try to black-mail the user into sabotaging me in some way."

"Like stealing," George added forcefully. "Or *breaking the law*."

"What was stolen?" Professor Frank asked, his tone still casual.

I glanced at George. "My father's legal files," I replied.

Professor Frank nodded. "And what was the outcome of that? Are the files still missing?"

I blushed. "Well . . . no," I replied. "They were scanned and returned. But UrNewReality posted them—they were confidential—in the game, on a movie screen in the mall."

The professor looked thoughtful. "And this cost your father money?" he asked. "Ruined his case?"

"Well—no," I stammered, trying to figure out where this conversation had gone wrong. "I mean—he could have been. It was just lucky. It just—"

"Who stole the files?" Professor Frank asked.

"Did they have reason to be upset with you, outside the game?"

I took a deep breath. "It was the girl who was cyberbullied," I said slowly. "And yes, she was a little upset with me. But that's—"

The professor cut me off. "What else was stolen?"

George's eyes were blazing. "My *laptop*," she said angrily. "Is that a big enough deal for you?"

The professor smiled, looking at George's lap. "You seem to be holding your laptop," he pointed out.

It was true. George had grabbed it on the way out of the car—she "didn't trust anybody" now.

George was turning bright red. "That's because we *caught* the *thief*," she replied through gritted teeth.

"Who was?" Professor Frank asked breezily, sitting back in his chair. "Your BF? Your BFF?"

George looked furious. "Hey—" she began to protest.

"Listen." Professor Frank leaned over his desk toward us, holding up his hand for silence. "I'm very sorry that you young ladies are having some problems with your friends. But really, what you're describing are petty teenage squabbles."

George gasped. "You—"

The professor held up his hand again. "If the game is causing such problems for you," he instructed, "it's really very simple. There is a magical button on your computer, called an Off button. Press it, and go outside, or read a book, or talk to your friends in person for once." He looked us both in the eye and leaned back in his chair. "Don't try to blame a piece of cutting-edge technology for your personal troubles."

George sat stiff beside me, sputtering. "I—well, just—you—"

I felt as angry as she sounded, but I had no idea what to say. Petty squabbles? Personal troubles? This man had no idea who he was talking to. I felt certain that he'd seen our young faces and assumed we were just a couple of silly teenagers.

"What about the hacking?" I asked finally, not moving from my chair. "Regardless of what's happened to us, doesn't it concern you that someone's hacked into the game, getting users' personal information?"

Professor Frank looked thoughtful, then shrugged. "Based on what you've told me, ladies, I'm not entirely sure someone *has* hacked the game. I think it's entirely possible that this UrNew-

Reality person is an angry friend of yours, someone who already had your contact info and is just
using the game to rattle you. But even so, experienced programmers aren't afraid of a little hacking.
Why, some of the most sophisticated technologi-
cal advances of our time have been instigated by
hackers. You don't—"

George slapped the edge of Professor Frank's
desk, cutting him off. I could see that she'd had
quite enough of this meeting. "Listen," she said.
"I don't care how silly you think we are. We're
not leaving this office until you give us Sung and
Crilley's contact information."

The professor still looked vaguely amused.
"Why?" he asked. "So they can concern themselves
with the trials and tribulations of some teenybopper feud?"

"No," said George, her voice steely, "so they
can be made aware that a hacker may be using
their game to break the law."

Professor Frank just stared at us for a moment.
His expression implied that he still thought we
both were ridiculous, but he also thought getting
us out of his office might be worth a phone call.
"All right," he said finally. "I'll call them myself.
I don't see any need to give out their personal
information to strangers."

"Good enough," George said with a shrug, tapping her index finger on the desk near the phone. "Let's make that call."

Professor Frank sighed. He looked from George to me, then pulled his chair over to the phone and picked up a PDA from the desk. Pressing a couple buttons and scrolling through, he seemed to find the information he needed and typed a number into the phone. I tried to memorize the numbers he was hitting, but the phone was at the wrong angle from both George and myself— I only caught a couple numbers.

After dialing, Professor Frank sat back in his chair and glanced at George. No one answered for a few seconds, and then the professor sat at attention as the call seemed to go to voicemail.

"Jack and Robert, hello," he began. "I'm sorry to bother you. I have two teenage girls in my office who seem very convinced that their recent personal troubles are due to a hacker getting into the BetterLife system." He chuckled. "Specifically, they think someone is using your program to steal personal information of other users. I know it sounds far-fetched. . . . Anyway, if you would like to reach this young lady, her name is—" He glanced up at George.

"George Fayne," she replied.

"George Fayne," the professor repeated. "And she can be reached at . . ."

George recited her cell phone number to the professor, and he repeated it into the phone. "Thank you!" he finished, and hung up the phone with a flourish.

"Well," he said to us, slowly rising from his chair, "this meeting has been most entertaining, but I think we're done here."

I glanced at George, nodding quickly. It was time for us to go. Clearly, that was all the help we were going to get out of the professor.

"Thank you," I said politely as I turned to the door.

"Yes—thank you," George added. Her tone was cold, and I wondered what she was thinking.

We walked out of the office quickly, and kept walking down the hall without a word. When we reached the cool, modern lobby of the computer science building, George turned to me.

"Can you *believe* that guy?"

"I know," I agreed, and just then my cell phone beeped that I had a text message. I pulled it out of my pocket and flipped it open. It was from Ned:

IS THAT GEORGE'S CAR I SEE IN PARKING LOT C?

I smiled, and quickly texted back:

WE'RE HERE TO MEET WITH PROFESSOR FRANK. COFFEE?

It took only seconds to get a reply.

STUDENT CENTER. BE THERE IN FIVE.

I looked up at George. "Let's talk about it over a cup of coffee with Ned," I suggested. "I don't know about you, but I could use something warm after that encounter."

"Tell me about it," George agreed, following me toward the student center with a nod. "That guy was cold as *ice*."

Ned was waiting for us with a table and three steaming lattes when we came to meet him at the student center. "I got you some drinks," he said, offering us two cups. "I thought you might need a caffeine fix."

"Thanks," George enthused, taking a long sip of her latte. "Ahhh. That's better."

I sat down and squeezed Ned's hand. "Thanks. We've had kind of a crazy morning."

Ned looked concerned. "What's up?"

Alternating stories and comments, George and

I filled Ned in on the morning's wild events: the library meeting that wasn't, the not-quite-thief Ibrahim, and the setup by someone at BetterLife—or someone who had hacked in to BetterLife.

"Wow," Ned murmured, shaking his head. "Poor Ibrahim! I had no idea any of this was going on with him."

George shot me an awkward look. In our recount to Ned, we'd downplayed Ibrahim's crush on me a little.

"What was in the e-mail that was so embarrassing?" he asked me.

"Oh, you know." I shrugged and sipped my latte again. "Typical teenager stuff."

George touched Ned's arm, jumping in to change the subject. "It gets worse," she promised. "Just now, Nancy and I had a meeting with Professor Frank, asking him to put us in touch with Jack Crilley and Robert Sung—you know, the BetterLife creators?"

Ned nodded. "Sure! Nancy and I saw them speak a few weeks ago. What did you need to tell them?"

"George wanted to warn them that someone was hacking into their game to steal users' personal information—like yours," I explained.

"It's a huge invasion of privacy for their users,"

George said. "I was sure they'd be upset about it."

Ned nodded, and I tried to look hopeful. "Maybe they will be, George, once they hear Professor Frank's voicemail."

George raised her eyebrows. "That's the thing," she said, leaning in confidentially and looking from Ned to me. "I didn't want to say anything before, but I'm not even entirely sure he really *called* Sung and Crilley."

I frowned. "You don't? But we were sitting right there while he did it."

"We were sitting right there," George confirmed, twirling her latte cup on the table, "but we didn't hear him actually *reach* anybody. We don't know for sure he got their voicemail. Heck, we don't even know for sure that he dialed a real phone number."

I bit my lip, considering this. Would Professor Frank be that brazen—faking a phone call to get rid of us?

"What makes you think that?" I asked George.

She shrugged. "I'm not totally sure, but I could swear I heard the dial tone when he was supposedly leaving a message." She sighed. "I couldn't say for certain, so I didn't say anything. But now I just have this terrible feeling he was playing with us."

I looked at Ned, who was looking mildly confused. "Professor Frank wasn't exactly rolling out the welcome mat for us," I explained.

"You can say that again," George added with a snort. Turning to Ned, she filled him in on some of the unsavory details of our conversation.

"Whoa!" cried Ned. "I would think he'd be a lot more interested in hacking and stealing personal information! I know he's a fan of the game, but wow. . . ."

"And it seems that he may not even have connected us to Sung and Crilley," I said with a sigh. "Up till now, I thought that awful conversation had at least been worth it. But now . . ."

I paused. And then, suddenly, it came to me.

"What if Professor Frank had a *reason* to dissuade us from pursuing our claims?" I asked.

George glanced up at me. I could see the light turning on in her eyes. "You mean . . ."

"He's a huge fan of BetterLife," I went on, "and obviously knows a lot about computer programming. If someone were to hack into the game— it would make sense for it to be an expert like him, no?"

George's jaw dropped. "And that would explain why he was just so nasty to us," she guessed. "If he *was* UrNewReality—why would he help us find him?"

"He saw me with Ned and Ibrahim at the lecture," I went on, "and I told Jack and Robert about Shannon, right in front of him. It wouldn't have been hard for him to look her up, especially if he knows his way around the game. . . ."

"Wait a minute, wait a minute," Ned broke in, holding up a hand to stop us. "He had the ability, sure—and I have to admit, it would make his behavior here make a lot more sense. But what's his motive?" he asked. "What could he have against you, Nancy?"

I swallowed. "I'm not sure," I admitted, then unleashed a huge grin. "And that, my friends, is why we're going to have to break into Professor Frank's office tonight to find out."

SNEAKY CHARACTERS

"I'm not sure I like this, Nancy." Ned, Bess, George and I were gathered in a small storage room next to the Seaver Hall cafeteria, pulling on our last pieces of black clothing.

"Come on, Ned," I urged, giving my boyfriend a reassuring pat. "We've been over this a hundred times. We've got the map of the tunnels under the campus, and you got that guest ID from your friend who works for campus security—we're all set."

Ned frowned. "I just hope we're not all set to be caught." He gulped, then looked at me. "You know midterms are coming up in two weeks, right? This is *not* the time for me to be caught sneaking into faculty offices."

"I thought you didn't have any classes with Professor Frank," Bess said, twirling her fluffy blond hair up into a messy bun and fixing a black baseball cap over it.

"I don't," Ned responded, "but I don't think that means I'm allowed to break into his office."

George shrugged. "I guess we'll have to check the R.H.U. honor code next time we have a chance."

When Ned shot her a look, she smiled.

"Come on, Ned. We'll be fine."

Ned took a deep breath and pulled a R.H.U. student ID out of his pocket. It wasn't his own ID, but a special ID marked "guest" that security gave visiting professors, potential students, or anyone who wanted to use certain university facilities without actually being enrolled here. With a final glance at us, he walked over to a heavy, locked metal door with a card reader to its right. He flashed the ID in front of the reader, and when it beeped in recognition, opened the door onto a dark stairway leading down.

Silently, Bess, George, and I followed Ned down the dark steps. We each carried a small flashlight, which we flicked on as soon as the door was shut behind us.

"Wow," Bess breathed, as the four of us arrived

at the bottom of the stairs—and a dark, empty tunnel, about ten feet wide and eight feet tall, stretched out in front of us. "How long have these tunnels been here?"

"Since the 1800s," Ned replied, "when the university was first built. Since then, they've been updated to connect to all the new buildings."

"And they were built to transport food?" I asked, looking around in amazement.

"Mostly," Ned replied. "They make it easier to move food from the cafeterias to big fancy events. But they also make it easier to set up the events themselves."

I glanced at George. "Have the map ready?"

"Yes indeed!" George smiled and unfurled a map that Ned had downloaded from a little-known university website. George had highlighted the route from the tunnel we were standing in to the tunnel that ran under the computer science center. According to the map, there was a door that would let us exit from the tunnel into a back corridor near some restrooms—and it should be easily accessible with our "guest" ID.

We walked swiftly through the tunnel, each beaming our flashlights ahead of us. We passed other tunnels connecting to different buildings, and stairways leading up to different points around campus. Every so often, we'd pass odd items stored in the tunnels: stacks of banquet tables or chairs, or the odd bookcase or desk. In the corners and dead ends, dust and cobwebs flourished. But in the main part of the tunnel, where we were traveling, the tunnel was clean and looked relatively well-traveled.

Suddenly, after we'd been walking for about fifteen minutes, Bess froze. "Do you hear that?"

I stopped too, biting my lip. "Hear what?"

But within a few seconds, the sound became clear. It was a rumbling sort of sound, followed by what sounded like the echo of a laugh.

"Are we near a building?" I asked urgently. "Could it be coming from above us?"

George consulted her map. "According to this, we're about a hundred yards from the nearest building," she replied. "Although, possibly, it could be coming from outs—"

RRRRRRRR. The sound was suddenly right behind us. We all whirled to face an offshoot of the tunnel we were in about twenty feet back. It sounded like somebody was wheeling a large cart or object right into our path. . . .

I almost shrieked as I felt a hand suddenly grab my shoulder. But I quickly realized it was just Ned, and he was trying to urge us to hide.

"We're not supposed to be down here," he whispered urgently. "Students aren't even supposed to know about these tunnels. I only heard about it from a friend who used to work in food service."

There was a door to our left—there seemed to be storage closets and electrical breakers scattered throughout the tunnels. Ned tried the handle, and miraculously, it opened. Inside, though, was a dark, creepy, dust-filled closet heaped with cobweb-covered furniture.

RRRRRR. Whoever was coming, they were even closer now.

Ned pushed us and we all dove into the closet. I sneezed immediately. I couldn't help it. I was pretty sure I was inhaling fifty years or more worth of dust. But fortunately, the cart or whatever it was made enough noise that I don't think anyone heard me. Ned pulled the door almost shut, so we had an inch or two to see out. A few seconds later, two janitors passed though, pushing a huge pallet of folding chairs on wheels.

"So then I said, I don't care how many things you've invented, buddy," the older janitor said to the younger, "you're going to need an ID if you want to . . ."

I breathed a sigh of relief. It seemed like they

hadn't seen us or even suspected anyone was there. After a few minutes—giving them enough time to get well ahead of us—we came back out, uselessly trying to brush all the dust off ourselves.

"When do you think that closet was last opened?" Bess asked with a sneeze.

George pointed to her map. "According to this, this part of the tunnels was built in 1934," she explained. "I'd guess around then."

Ned glanced around nervously. "Let's go, girls," he suggested. "I don't want any more close calls."

We made our way through the remainder of the tunnels quickly, and thankfully, we didn't see or hear anyone else. We had to take a few turns, taking legs of different tunnels leading in different directions, but finally George announced that we were under the computer science center.

She gestured to a small tunnel off to the right that led to a relatively modern-looking staircase. "If we go up there and open the door, we should be in a hallway with a storage closet and a pair of restrooms off the computer lab. Hopefully we won't run into anybody."

I nodded, and we all proceeded down the tunnel and up the stairs. At the top of the stairs, Ned swiped his Guest ID through another card reader, and the door opened. We all silently piled out into a surprisingly bright, clean, modern corridor.

"All right," I whispered. "Now we just need to get to Professor Frank's office without being seen."

Unfortunately, it seemed that the corridor we were in led right to the student computer lab. We probably could have passed for students—were it not for the ridiculous all-black costumes we were wearing. (Bess thought they would be "better for sneaking" than regular clothes.)

We crept closer to the lab. Two students were inside, chatting over a state-of-the-art computer.

"I just don't want to make the wrong decision," the first student said, a young Indian girl with long, perfectly straight, inky black hair.

"I know," her cohort agreed, a tall freckled boy about the same age with flaming red hair and glasses. "Your choice here will either impress him, or make you look like you haven't been listening at all."

The girl nodded. "It's just, I'm not sure what would make the most sense. . . ."

George smiled, turning back to us. "They must be working on some really big assignment," she said.

Just then, a familiar noise came from the computer—the telltale *beep* that told you you had a message in BetterLife.

"Oh, my God," the girl said. "I cannot *believe* he would say that to KafkaLover45! That's it, she's breaking up with him. I don't care about his big plans to open a virtual pet store at the virtual mall."

I turned to George. "They're playing Better-Life."

She sighed. "Well, that's good for us," she said, sneaking out into the open a little. "They're so engrossed in the game, it should be easy for us to slip right by."

And so it was. The girl and her friend never even glanced up from the screen, where it seemed KafkaLover45's boyfriend was not taking the breakup well. We easily ran by and ran up the flight of stairs that would lead us to the offices of the computer science department.

It was late, so the upstairs offices were completely empty. George and I easily pointed the way to Professor Frank's office, where we'd had our unpleasant conversation earlier that day. Bess examined the lock, and after some deliberation, she grabbed a paper clip off the department secretary's desk and bent it into a long, straight wire.

"That looks pretty high-tech, there," George teased her.

Bess just smirked. "Not everything has to have a hard drive and a charger, Ms. I-Eat-Computers-for-Breakfast."

Carefully, she inserted the wire into the lock, wiggled it a few times, and then we heard a *click*.

"Voila!" Bess whispered with a smile, turning the knob and opening the door to Professor Frank's office. "Easy as pie."

"Thanks, guys," I said, shooting grateful glances at Bess, George, and Ned. "I know I couldn't have done this without your help."

Bess smiled, flicking on the light. "I think we're okay using this, yeah?" she asked. "This whole part of the building seems pretty deserted."

I nodded. "I think it's okay, but let's make this snappy. Divide and conquer! Ned, you take the filing cabinet; Bess, you take the bookshelves; George, you're on his computer, of course."

George grinned. "Of course."

"And I'll tackle the desk," I added, allowing George to get by me to get to the computer. "Now let's get some evidence!"

For a few minutes, we all just dug, each of us searching our appointed location for *anything* that might give Professor Frank a reason for harassing me or my friends. I was hoping that everyone else was having better luck, because my search of Frank's desk merely turned up a Dilbert day calendar (almost blank—my guess was that he entered his appointments into the calendar on his computer), a photo of three completely normal-looking children, and some department memos and programming papers, none of which seemed to relate to our case at all.

But then George spoke up. "This is weird," she observed. I turned to see that she had called up the Internet browser and was on the professor's BetterLife login page. "It looks like Professor Frank has not one, not two, but *eight* different avatars on BetterLife."

"Wow," Bess murmured. "Well, we know from the lecture that he really likes the program."

"But the weird thing," George went on, "is that the avatars are all completely different ages, genders, 'types'—and he's playing in several different worlds. Some we've come across in our research the last few weeks, but some I've *never* heard of." She paused. "Did you know there was a *Star Wars* fans world on BetterLife? Or a world just for insurance salesmen?"

I frowned. "You're telling me he has an insurance salesman avatar so he can go online and pretend to be an insurance salesman, among other insurance salesmen?"

George nodded. "But that's not even the weirdest. He has a thirteen-year-old girl avatar named PrincessF that he uses in the middle school forums. He has a high school avatar too, and several university avatars." Suddenly she gasped.

"What is it?" I asked, drawing closer to the computer.

"And he has this avatar," she showed me, leaning back from the computer. I moved closer and gasped.

"Oh my gosh."

The screen showed a sort of profile of the professor's most recently-created avatar—GuitarLvr15. The avatar looked exactly like Rebecca's had, with a blue streak in his hair and punky clothing. The avatar looked just like the barista at Rebecca's favorite coffee shop that both she and Shannon had been crushing on. It was almost eerie to see him again. Somehow, the professor had gotten all of the details of Rebecca's creation and re-created him, this time under his control.

"It *was* him," I breathed. There could be no question now: The message with my dad's private files had come from Professor Frank.

"Professor Frank?" a voice suddenly called from

the hallway. "Professor Frank? Are you there?"

My friends and I all looked at each other and froze. Who could be looking for Professor Frank this late at night? Wordlessly, Bess clicked off the office light, and we all scrambled for a place to hide—all ending up behind Professor Frank's huge desk. (There just weren't many good hiding options in his office.)

"Professor Frank?" the voice called again, drawing closer. I recognized it now as the same girl who'd been breaking up with her BetterLife boyfriend downstairs. "I could really use some advice on what to do now that SoupMan and I are broken up. I was thinking I should start a new avatar, but I wanted to ask you about the *Star Wars* . . ."

She trailed off suddenly, now close outside the office.

"I could have sworn that office light was on," she muttered, then we heard her turn and walk back down the hall she'd come from. "*Losing* it . . ."

Slowly, after a few seconds, the four of us reanimated. This time we just flicked on our flashlights, though, and didn't turn on the office light.

"His students come to him for advice on *Better-Life*?" George asked wonderingly.

"I think we've established," I said, still reeling

from the revelation that Professor Frank really was GuitarLvr15, "that he's kind of obsessed with the game."

"And there's more," Ned added, standing up to grab something from the top of the filing cabinet. "I just found this while you guys were checking him out on BetterLife."

He handed me a sheet of paper. It was written on BetterLife Inc. stationery; that caught my eye right away. And as I read through the letter, my jaw dropped.

"It's a letter from Robert Sung," I whispered to Bess and George, "*thanking* him for his recent investment of twenty-five thousand dollars in their subscription-service plan!"

Bess gasped. "No!"

"Yeah," I confirmed, reading through the rest. "Wow. Well, guys, this is our motive. If Professor Frank was a huge investor in BetterLife, and needs the subscription plan to succeed . . ."

". . . then of *course* he would want to squash any perceived threats to the brand," George finished, shaking her head. "Like you, and your questions about security, and your accusations of cyberbullying. Which explains why he was such a pill to us this afternoon. And why he probably just mimed calling Robert Sung and Jack Crilley to get rid of us."

I nodded. "Exactly." I had to admit, it didn't quite seem real. Professor Frank was clearly Guitar-Lvr15—but did that mean he was UrNewReality too? It seemed likely, but something still didn't compute. Why would he bother using two avatars? Just to throw me off? That was definitely possible. And, I had to admit to myself as I looked over the professor's scattered belongings, it seemed most likely. "Well," I said, arranging the professor's desk items back in their original places. "I guess we're done here. We can go."

My friends nodded, also seeming a little stunned by how neatly this had all come together, and began restoring their own areas to look like we'd never been there. Suddenly, the silence was cut by a loud, electronic musical tone. We all jumped.

"Sorry!" George said, sheepishly fishing her PDA out of her pocket. "I didn't think anyone would call me this late."

She quickly answered it, silencing the loud ring. "Hello?" she said, looking a little non-plussed, like she expected a telemarketer.

But it clearly wasn't a telemarketer. Her eyes

widened as her caller spoke, and she looked straight at me.

"Oh yes," she said politely, her expression turning to utter confusion. "I really appreciate your calling me back, *Mr. Crilley*."

AN UNEXPECTED ADVENTURE

"**S**o what did he say?" Bess asked eagerly as we all sat in my Prius at a McDonald's parking lot a few blocks from the campus. (I'd wanted to get away from the university before discussing; even though we'd gotten away with it, I still worried that someone might notice that it was odd we were all wearing black and covered with dust.)

George shook her head. "He said he was horrified to learn that someone had hacked into his precious baby, and he wanted to solve the issue right away. He and his partner are in town tomorrow for an appearance to celebrate the subscription plan launch at the Gaming Garage on River Street. He wants us to meet up with him tomorrow morning, a few hours before their appearance." She looked at me and shrugged. George seemed to be more confused by this phone call than ever.

"Another 'meeting'?" I asked skeptically. "I don't know. How do we know it was really him that you were talking to?"

"It sounded like him," George replied, looking thoughtful. "And he was throwing out a lot of technical jargon. If it wasn't him, it was someone who knows a lot about computers, and the program."

"Well, the hacker would know all that stuff, right?" Ned asked.

George sighed. "He or she would," she agreed. "I really think it was him, though. He sounded just like he does on the news. And we can easily check whether Sung and Crilley are appearing at the Gaming Garage tomorrow," she said, holding up her PDA.

I nodded. George quickly pressed a bunch of buttons, and soon seemed to be scrolling through a website. "Here it is," she said cheerfully. "'Jack Crilley and Robert Sung sign autographs and discuss the new BetterLife subscription service, one p.m., Gaming Garage, River Heights.'" She looked up at us. "It's definitely worth a trip by. If we keep our wits about us."

I nodded slowly. George was right, but I was feeling preoccupied by what all this meant. "So wait a minute," I said. "If it really was Crilley, that means Professor Frank really did call him."

Bess nodded, tapping her lips with her finger. "It's strange, right?" she asked. "If he really called—is there any chance we got what we found tonight wrong?"

Ned frowned. "Well, just because he really called him doesn't mean he can't be Guitarlvr15—or UrNewReality, for that matter," he said. "Maybe you guys frustrated him enough that he called to get rid of you. Or maybe he thought Crilley would blow you off."

"He definitely invested in the subscription service," Bess went on. "And he's *definitely* Guitarlvr15. We saw the proof on his computer. That's enough to be pretty incriminating, right there."

I nodded, still thinking this through. "If that's the case," I said finally, "then we should go to the police. They should know about this."

I looked around at my friends' faces. They all looked as hesitant as I was feeling. It wasn't that the River Heights police force weren't nice, or wouldn't try to help us. . . . I just wondered how much of this whole cyberbullying thing they would understand.

"All right," Ned said, clapping his hands together with a determined expression. "Off to the police." He glanced around at the rest of us, as if assessing whether we were ready. No matter what happened, we were in for a long night.

"Off to the police," George agreed.

"Right," Bess added with a yawn.

"Off to the police," I said finally, putting the car into gear with a sigh.

Three hours later, Ned and I headed home from the university, where we'd dropped Bess and George at their cars, with a couple of huge yawns. Our meeting with the River Heights police had been long and confusing, requiring lots of explanations and demonstrations with the computer, but it seemed to have worked. They'd agreed to bring Professor Frank in for questioning the next morning, at least. And they seemed to understand that this was a serious crime. I could only hope that their interview with Professor Frank would give us the explanations we needed.

"Well, this has been quite a night," Ned said, leaning back in the passenger seat. "I feel like we have more questions than answers. Don't you?"

"Yeah," I agreed sleepily, the streetlights all starting to blend together in my vision. "I wish this case had clearer answers. But everything just seems to lead to another question."

"Maybe it's because it all leads back to the Internet," Ned suggested. "And like everyone keeps telling us, on the Internet you can be whoever you want."

"Even a criminal," I agreed.

"Even a criminal," Ned echoed. "In fact, it seems like being a criminal is very easy on BetterLife."

A musical tone suddenly chimed, like the sound my computer made when it booted up. Ned pulled out his PDA. "I have an e-mail," he said, looking at his phone in surprise. "Who'd be e-mailing me at this hour? *Oh.*"

I turned to glance at him, and found him staring into the screen on his PDA with furrowed brows. "What is it, Ned?"

"It's not an e-mail," Ned replied, looking a little hesitant to share the rest. "It's a message from BetterLife. After I got the message from UrNew-Reality, I turned on their special alert service where you can have messages e-mailed to you."

I paused at a stop sign, then turned and looked at him. "Ned?" I said, my heart speeding up. "Is it a message from who I think it is?"

Ned looked at the screen, then back at me. "It's UrNewReality."

I glanced in the rearview mirror. There was no one behind me; the streets were as deserted as you might expect at 2 a.m. on a weeknight. I kept my foot on the brakes. "Let me see."

Looking a little reluctant, Ned handed his PDA over. I read:

FROM: URNEWREALITY
TO: NATTYNED145
UNR IS READY FOR UR HELP. IF U WANT UR SECRETS
KEPT U WILL MEET UNR NOW @ THE * ON THE ATTACHED
MAP. UNR WILL GIVE U DETAILS THEN.
COME ALONE!!

"Oh, my gosh!" I breathed excitedly, feeling the sleepiness of the last few hours fade away. "What does the map say?"

"I didn't even look, Nance," Ned replied, taking back his phone with a distinctly unenthusiastic expression. "It's two o'clock in the morning! We have no idea who this person is or what they want! Besides, aren't we pretty sure we know who's behind this whole thing?"

I sighed. "We know Professor Frank was Guitarlvr15," I replied, "but someone else could be behind the messages from UrNewReality. Or he could have accomplices. . . . Ned, we *have* to go where the map tells us! We could finally see the face behind the threats!"

Ned shook his head. "Nance . . ." he began. But I could tell he was already wearing down.

"Come on," I urged. "We'll go together, keep each other safe. I'll trail you, just out of sight, and we can keep in touch by text message. Ned, we can finally catch this guy! I can finally use my computer again, without worrying what e-mails UrNewReality is going to try to use against me or which of my friends he's going to go after next!"

Ned sighed. He looked out the window. "I think this could be a bad idea," he said. "We're both tired. And we have no idea who we're dealing with. It could be Professor Frank or some harmless kid . . . or it could be a whole gang of guys! Whoever UrNewReality is, they're clearly willing to break the law."

I nodded. "That's why we'll be careful."

Ned frowned, still staring out the window.

"Ned," I said gently. "Please. This has kind of taken over my life these last few days. I *have* to find out who's really behind all these threats."

Ned was silent for a few seconds. Finally, he let out a huge sigh. "Fine," he agreed in a reluctant tone.

I leaned over and wrapped my arms around him. "Thank you," I said sincerely.

He took my hand and squeezed it. "We'll find this guy, Nance," he said with a little smile. "And then we'll finally get some sleep."

The map attached to Ned's message directed us to Kelley Park, a long stretch of hiking trails, tennis courts, a public pool, and a small swimming beach down by the river. The park was huge, and the hiking trails wound through acres and acres of untamed woods. It was, quite honestly, kind of a creepy place to meet someone in the middle of the night.

I parked my Prius down the street from the park's southern border rather than drive all the way in and park in the parking lot. "You walk in first, and I'll follow about fifty yards behind you," I told Ned. "That way, it'll look like you arrived alone on foot. It won't look as suspicious as having you get out of the passenger seat of a strange car."

Ned looked a little unsure. "Are you sure this is a good idea, Nancy?" he asked, looking me in the eye. "The message couldn't have been clearer. They wanted me to *come alone.*"

I nodded. "I'll be careful, Ned. I promise. After

133

all the crazy stuff I've been through, I know how to take care of myself."

Ned sighed. "I know you do. I'm just wondering, in this case, if it's worth the risk."

I looked into Ned's brown eyes and touched his arm. "Ned, I've never been closer to actually seeing the person who's been harassing me all this time. It is *definitely* worth the risk. I'll be careful. You know I can run like heck. Okay?"

Ned sighed again and nodded, not meeting my eyes. "Okay," he agreed, and stepped out of the car.

Holding his PDA in his left hand, Ned ambled to the park's south entrance. The message he'd received had directed him to go to a picnic area on the park's east side. From here, he would have to walk fairly far, but I figured that was better than possibly letting UrNewReality see us arrive in my Prius.

Shortly after Ned disappeared down the dark trail leading into the park, I opened my own door and stepped out. Taking a good look all around me, I grabbed my own cell phone, softly closed the door, and began following Ned.

I sent him a quick text:

OK SO FAR?

He wrote back within seconds.

ALL CLEAR.

It took about fifteen minutes to walk from the south entrance to the park to the picnic area indicated on the map. The woods were very dark, and the new moon that night did little to illuminate the path in front of me. Still, I didn't dare turn on my flashlight, for fear of drawing attention. I just walked slowly and carefully, feeling in front of me with my hands and making sure the ground was level before putting weight on my feet. It was slow going, but I could see I was making progress. I passed tennis courts on my left, and then a hand-carved wooden sign told me that I was three tenths of a mile from the picnic site.

Beep! I startled, then grabbed my cell phone and hit the Vibrate button. I couldn't believe I'd forgotten to silence it! Onscreen, I had a new text from Ned:

I'M HERE.

I texted back:

I'M RIGHT BEHIND YOU.

But just as I hit the Send button, my phone vibrated with another text. I glanced at the screen.

FORWARDED BY NED NICKERSON
FROM *314-555-6723*
GOOD JOB. U FOLLOW DIRECTIONS. NOW COME TO THE BOATHOUSE.

I took a deep breath. The phone number had to be UrNewReality's cell. He or she must've gotten Ned's cell number from his Internet records. And they were playing with him; whoever UrNew-Reality was, they were making Ned work for his assignment. Was it worth playing along?

I didn't love the idea of a scavenger hunt through Kelley Park at two o'clock in the morning. But I was even more turned off by the idea of being this close to UrNewReality, and letting him or her get away.

I texted Ned back:

LET'S GO.

He responded seconds later:

OK.

The boathouse, of course, was on the river, near the swimming beach. It didn't house boats so much as canoes and kayaks, which you could rent by the hour. It was another good half mile down the trail from the picnic area. Squinting to search the ground in front of me, I crossed the picnic area and ducked onto the trail marked with another hand-carved sign: BOATHOUSE, ½ MILE.

It was another dark, difficult walk through the woods. This time, my foot actually caught on a root at one point, and I went flying, stopping short on my knees at the very last minute. Good thing, too, because the path was littered with stones, and I realized that had I fallen any farther my head would have smacked into a pretty big one. I sat up and took a breath, my heart pounding, full of adrenaline. I felt wide awake now. And even angrier at UrNewReality than I ever had been before.

A few minutes after my fall, I had recovered myself and was almost to the boathouse. My phone vibrated in my hand.

NANCE. THEY WANT ME TO JUMP IN THE RIVER.

What? I wondered. It was a cold night. Why on earth would they want . . . But then my phone vibrated again.

FORWARDED BY NED NICKERSON
FROM 314-555-6723
GOOD JOB. C THE FLOAT N THE RIVER? THAT'S UR NEXT
CLUE.

My phone vibrated one more time, this time with another text from Ned:

I THINK THIS IS A BAD IDEA.

My heart jumped in my chest. *No! We can't stop now.* I swallowed and took a deep breath, trying to think over this rationally. I texted back:

LOOK IN THE BOATHOUSE. IS THERE ANYTHING YOU CAN
USE TO GET IT?

As I waited for Ned to text me back, my mind was racing. Could I jump in the river for him, to retrieve it? Or could I kayak over to it? Not really; not without looking obvious. After all, if UrNew-Reality was texting Ned the moment he arrived at a location, clearly they were watching him—a thought that made me feel a little squirmy.

My phone vibrated.

FOUND A NET. HANG ON. . . .

And a few seconds later:

GOT IT. SAYS TO GO TO THE WEST PARKING LOT.

The west parking lot. That was pretty far away, by the tennis courts. It was also in a pretty secluded part of the park, near more hiking and preserved forest, far from the road. As much as I wanted to find this person, my stomach did a little flip. Was this safe? What if Ned had jumped in the water to get the clue, and something had happened to him? I didn't get the feeling that UrNewReality was exactly concerned about my boyfriend's well-being. He or she was only worried about what Ned could do—presumably, to help complicate my life.

But we were so close. I texted Ned back.

LET'S GO.

It took a few seconds for Ned to answer this time.

OK. BE CAREFUL NANCY.

I will, I silently promised myself. *We both will.* Following the signs, I found another trail, which thankfully was paved and a little wider than the trails we'd taken so far. Ned had taken a flashlight, since he was *supposed* to be there—it was no big deal if UrNewReality spotted him walking through the woods. Looking ahead on the trail, which was almost straight, I could see a warm yellow light in the distance, framing Ned's figure. I followed behind, allowing myself to get just a little closer than fifty yards. I hoped we were almost finished. I worried that this could go on indefinitely: reach the location, get another text. Reach the location, get another text. Like some kind of test of Ned's endurance.

We walked for what seemed like hours, but was probably only another twenty minutes. I could hear animals in the woods, owls and something scurrying through the bushes—probably squirrels and chipmunks. Every so often, there would be a sound I couldn't identify, which I told myself was just wind through the trees. My eyes had almost completely adjusted to the lack of light, but I was beginning to feel tired again. My eyes felt droopy.

Suddenly my phone vibrated.

OK. I'M HERE. NOTHING.

My heart sank. *Nothing*? Could UrNewReality be completely playing with Ned, leading him to a dead end?

I quickened my pace as the phone vibrated again.

WAIT. BLACK SUV IN DISTANCE.

I swallowed. That had to be UrNewReality— right? I texted back:

EMPTY?

Ned replied right away:

CAN'T TELL. DARK WINDOWS.

Just then, I heard a car starting up. I wasn't very far now, and it was clearly coming from the parking lot.

My phone vibrated.

HEADLIGHTS ON. COMING TOWARD ME!

My heart raced. Was Ned in danger? I clutched my phone in my hand and started running. But

I only got a few feet before my phone vibrated again, and I had to stop to see what Ned was telling me.

THEY WANT ME TO GET IN THE CAR.

They want me to get in the car. They want me to get in the car. I stared at the screen for a few seconds as the words echoed in my mind. Should he get in the car? If he did, he would find out for sure who UrNewReality is. And Ned was smart; he knew not to go anywhere with these people. Assuming that UrNewReality was more than one person. He had said *they,* I realized.

Could Ned defend himself against more than one person?

I heard footsteps up ahead and my heart jumped into my chest. Suddenly it just seemed all wrong, and I realized how incredibly dangerous this was. *They want me to get in the car.* That could mean anything; this whole hunt through the woods was already much more involved than what they'd asked of Shannon or Ibrahim. Did they know that Ned was my boyfriend? Were they saving the worst punishment for him?

I gulped, torn between running or texting. I was far enough away that even running, it would be a minute or two before I reached Ned. I clutched my phone and frantically texted back, not caring that I hit all the wrong buttons or keys. . . .

DOMT GO!! DON'T GP!!!!!

I hit Send and started running. "Ned! Ned!" I called, not caring who heard me. I heard car doors slam and an engine rev up. Then I heard a car peel out.

When I finally reached the lot, the first thing I noticed was that Ned was gone. In fact, everything was gone. The lot seemed dark and deserted.

That's when I heard the engine rev up again. From the far left side of the lot, headlights illuminated and trained on me. I stood frozen as the huge SUV hurtled in my direction.

Move! Move! Move! My mind screamed, and finally, with just seconds to spare, I forced my frozen legs to jump out of the way.

The SUV screeched by me, the back passenger window still half open—and through it, Ned's face, looking stunned and frightened. "Nance!" he cried as a hand came from behind him and pushed the automatic window button, forcing the darkened glass up.

Someone punched the gas, and the SUV sped out of the parking lot. For the next few seconds, all I could hear was the grinding engine as it grew more and more distant.

Then my phone vibrated again. It was a text from Ned's phone.

I TOLD HIM TO COME ALONE, NANCY DREW.

I felt my blood turn to ice.

After that, no matter how many times I texted or called, nobody answered.

REAL-LIFE CRIME

"**O**hmigosh, Nancy!" Bess came running into the lobby of the River Heights police station, her cheeks pink, closely trailed by George. Their faces radiated concern as they ran over to where I sat huddled in an orange plastic chair. A cold, tasteless cup of coffee sat on a table next to me, and I clutched an ancient tissue in my hand that had been soaked with tears, dried, and then soaked again.

I think it's safe to say I was a mess.

"Are you okay?" George asked as she and Bess flanked my chair. "Did you sleep at all? Did they find out anything?"

I swallowed, and my throat burned. I took a

sip of the disgusting coffee to cool it. "No," I replied, my throat raspy. "On all counts."

It was ten o'clock in the morning, and I'd spent the night with the RHPD. I'd spent hours telling them all the details of Ned's disappearance, only to be told that he wasn't considered "missing" yet—and that, because he was a college student and they keep odd hours and played weird pranks, the police weren't completely convinced there was any foul play involved here.

"Is there any chance he knew the people in the SUV?" Officer Carr had asked me, looking concerned but skeptical. "Could this be a game or a practical joke? We deal with lots of hijinks at the university, Nancy."

My jaw had dropped. I knew the River Heights Police could be a little slow to get moving on a case before, but this was the first time their lack of interest was turned against me. "You don't know Ned," I'd replied, shaking my head. "He would never play a joke like that on me. He's always honest and straightforward! And he was exhausted by the time we got to the park."

Officer Carr had sighed. "It's not that I don't believe you, Nancy," he'd said. "But you know we have to wait twenty-four hours."

Now George and Bess watched me with concerned expressions. "What happened, exactly?" Bess asked.

I launched into the story: the message Ned had received on BetterLife, my bright idea to try and track UrNewReality down, and the scavenger hunt through the woods. And finally, the mysterious black SUV that had taken Ned away.

Bess and George looked just as worried as I felt. "What was the number they were texting you from?" George asked, pulling out her PDA.

I took out my cell phone and showed her.

George brought up a Web browser on her PDA and, in a few short clicks, plugged the phone number into a reverse cell phone directory. I began to feel a little better. Already, George was doing more for me than the police had. But when the results came up, George just sighed and shook her head. "There's no name associated with that number," she told me. "Which probably means it's a disposable cell phone. Perfect for sending anonymous messages and making anonymous calls."

I nodded, disappointed, but not surprised. Whoever UrNewReality was, he or she certainly knew a lot about remaining anonymous. "Oh well."

Bess frowned. "Nancy, maybe we should contact the local hospitals?" she asked. "Is there any chance Ned might have turned up . . ."

I shook my head. "I'm way ahead of you," I replied. "I called all of the area hospitals a few minutes ago. Nobody meeting Ned's description came in." I sighed. "And I called Ned's parents. They're on their way here. I told them the police were refusing to investigate unless Ned is still missing tonight, but Mrs. Nickerson thought maybe if they came down here, they could convince the police otherwise."

George nodded, glancing at the officer behind the reception desk, who was staring into his lap and doing his best to pretend he wasn't hearing our conversation. "Good luck with that," George murmured.

Just then, a *BEEP!* sounded from George's PDA. Bess and I looked at her expectantly as George glanced at the screen and then pressed a few buttons.

"Is it a message?" Bess asked eagerly. "UrNewReality again?"

George shook her head. "Nothing that exciting, I'm afraid." She looked at me. "It's my calendar feature, reminding me that we have a meeting with Jack Crilley in half an hour."

I groaned, rubbing my eyes. Of course I'd completely forgotten in all the excitement.

"Do you want to cancel?" George asked. "You'd

be totally justified, under the circumstances."

I shook my head. "No. If we want to keep this from happening to any other BetterLife users, we need to meet with Jack Crilley. Besides, I think I've done all I can here. Let me just run home and change clothes, and we can go to the Gaming Garage."

Bess and George nodded sympathetically and stepped back as I stood up. Just then, two officers came in the front door of the police station. I recognized them as the pair that had left to question Professor Frank just an hour before.

"Well?" I asked them, moving to block their path to the back offices. "What did Professor Frank tell you?"

The younger officer, who hadn't interacted with me at all before, glanced at his partner warily: Who was this nosy teenager? But the older officer gave him a look that said, *She's okay.* He turned to me.

"Funny thing," he announced. "Professor Frank wasn't home."

That seemed odd. "At nine o'clock in the morning?" I asked. "That's before office hours. Did you leave him a note?"

The officer glanced again at his partner and sighed. "Not exactly," he replied. "In fact . . . there were some odd things about Professor Frank's absence."

Odd things? My crime antennae went flying up. "What odd things?"

"Well, for one," the younger officer told me, "his front door was wide open, and his wallet and cell phone were still sitting on his kitchen counter."

I swallowed. That was *very* odd. Who left home without locking the door and bringing their wallet?

"Also," the older officer added, "there were signs of a struggle. The phone was knocked off the wall in the kitchen, and a glass was smashed on the floor."

My insides froze. What the officers were describing didn't sound at all like an eccentric man wandering off for a morning stroll. What they were describing sounded like foul play—*very* foul.

"Someone took him," I said, giving voice to my worst feelings. "Someone kidnapped him. He didn't leave under his own power." *And that means Ned is in even worse danger than I thought,* I added mentally. *If Professor Frank is missing, then he definitely isn't UrNewReality. And if UrNewReality is crazy enough to take them both . . .*

The officers looked at each other, clearly

uncomfortable. "It's something we still need to look into," the older one said.

I sighed, frustrated, and turned back to my friends. "Let's go." I was more determined now to meet with Jack Crilley than ever. Something very fishy was going on in BetterLife, and the stakes were getting higher and higher! This went way beyond teenage hijinks, as Professor Frank might have called them, or even cyberbullying—this was real-life kidnapping. I just hoped it wouldn't turn into something worse.

As we were walking out the front door, I spotted Mrs. Nickerson running through the parking lot toward the station. "Nancy!" she cried when she saw me, wrapping her arms around me in a comforting hug. "We called Carson to fill him in, but he said you'd already called him. Are you all right? Have you been here all night?"

I nodded sleepily and filled Mrs. Nickerson in on the latest developments—everything I'd told the police about Ned, and what I'd just learned about Professor Frank.

"I have to go for an hour or so," I told Mrs. Nickerson. "I need to go home and shower, and I have a meeting that I really can't miss. But then I'll be back here."

Mrs. Nickerson touched my head. "Nancy,

that's not necessary," she said gently. "I'll do what I can. You can get some sleep."

I shook my head. "I'm not going to be able to sleep until Ned is safe and sound and back with us," I insisted.

Mrs. Nickerson smiled sadly, reaching to take my hand and squeeze it. "That makes two of us," she told me.

A quick shower, a change of clothes, and a huge cup of coffee later, George, Bess, and I pulled up to the Gaming Garage. I had never been there before, but George had; it was a huge hangout spot for video gamers and technophiles like her. She explained that they had a huge gaming area where local gamers met up and held competitions, and they hosted several statewide and even national gaming championships. "It's a big deal," she told me. "Gamers love this place."

We climbed out of my Prius and stared at the entrance. Oddly enough, it seemed to be deserted this morning. Ours was the only car parked near the entrance, though a couple others hovered at the edges of the lot, near a neighboring mini-mall.

"It seems kind of empty," I observed.

George just shrugged. "Well, it's early," she

replied. "Gamers don't tend to be a big out-of-bed-at-dawn kind of crowd."

We walked up to the front door. Inside, fluorescent lights illuminated rows upon rows of video and computer games, along with the latest gaming systems and equipment. A huge sign was posted in the front window: MEET BETTER-LIFE CREATORS ROBERT SUNG AND JACK CRILLEY HERE AT 1 PM SATURDAY! But inside, it looked pretty deserted. In fact, when Bess pushed on the front door, it wouldn't budge.

She turned to us with a confused expression. "It's . . . closed?" she asked.

George pointed to a sign that read HOURS, scrolling down to find SATURDAY. "'Noon till 11 p.m.,'" she read. "Uh-oh. I think it is closed."

I groaned. "If we've been set up by these people *again* . . ."

But just then, George's phone beeped. She pulled it out of her pocket and glanced at the screen. "Text message," she told us. Pressing a couple buttons, she opened the message and held it up to show us:

SRY, THEY OFFERED TO OPEN EARLY 4 US—ENTER CODE 5-6-9-3 TO GET IN.

"Enter code?" I repeated. "Enter code where? I don't understand."

Bess reached out and grabbed a small dial high up on the front door. "I'm guessing here," she replied. "It looks like a combination lock."

George nodded, still glancing at her phone. "Well, give it a shot."

Bess spun the dial and entered the four numbers—5-9-6-3. It took a few seconds, but then a chime sounded and we heard the lock disengage. Bess pushed the door again, and this time it opened easily.

"Wow," she said, with a smile aimed at George. "Modern technology."

George just grinned. "How about that."

Bess entered the store, with George and me close behind.

Now inside, I realized that only the lights nearest the door were on—the rest of the store was dark and, it appeared, empty. "Hello?" I called. My voice echoed in the cavernous space, but no one responded. "Hello?"

George looked around. "Maybe we should head to the gaming room," she suggested. "It's through these aisles, in back."

I shrugged. "Sounds good to me."

We all walked through the dark, eerily silent

aisles to an open rear door. The room inside appeared dark, but as we grew closer I could hear *bleeps* and *bloops* coming from inside—the telltale sounds of a video game. As we walked up to the door, I caught sight of several huge plasma televisions mounted on the wall. It was dark inside except for the televisions, but I could just make out several rows of big, cushy leather chairs that faced the screens a few yards in front of us. George had been right—this place was a gamer's paradise.

"Hello?" I called again.

Virtual car horns and traffic noises were my only reply.

"He's probably really into his game," George suggested. "Let's just go in."

The chairs were too tall for us to tell if they were occupied, so I figured George was right—Robert Sung and Jack Crilley were probably sitting in the front row, enjoying a game of their incredibly popular creation. In fact, I now recognized some of the fake traffic and "outdoor" noise as coming from Virtual River Heights.

Feeling a little bit of sensory overload, I walked into the flashing, bleeping, blooping room, flanked by my two friends. The gaming room was windowless, and I could tell that the sound system was state-of-the-art. I imagined it might be very easy to settle down into one of those chairs and forget the outside world for a few hours.

When we were a few yards from the heavy metal door, it swung shut behind us. There was no window, so the closed door cut off every last bit of daylight that had crept into the store. We were completely surrounded by Virtual River Heights.

Then there was a loud "clicking" sound. Bess gave me a worried glance, then ran back a few feet to try the door. She turned back to us in shock. "It's locked," she whispered. "We're locked in here."

Just as my hackles started to rise, George's phone beeped. She swallowed and glanced at the screen. "Text message." Pressing a couple buttons, she brought up a text from the same number as before:

LOG ON TO THE COMPUTER.

"Why would they lock us in here?" Bess asked. "Who even did it? The store was empty."

"Maybe they just want our full attention," I suggested, but deep down I was just as disturbed by this development as Bess was. "Maybe it's for security's sake? They don't want anyone else hearing trade secrets?"

"Hello?!" George called into the cavernous room, but there was no reply. Slowly, we approached the gaming chairs. As we got closer, it was clear that each one was empty. I blinked and looked up at the largest plasma television I'd ever seen, mounted directly in front of us. I realized now that the screen was set to the BetterLife login page. The *bleeps, bloops,* and virtual street noise we'd heard before were just part of the looping street scene that enticed users to log in.

I walked to the front row of chairs. Each chair was equipped with a full keyboard, mouse, and gaming control. When I lifted the mouse, the arrow onscreen moved. I clicked on the Username box and the cursor appeared.

I looked back at George and Bess.

"What's going on?" Bess asked.

This was not at all what I'd pictured. I'd thought we'd have a simple sit-down with Jack and Robert; we'd tell them what we knew, they would thank us, and I'd run back to the police station. I had no idea that we'd end up locked in this gaming room, communicating with who-knows-who through a video game. But . . .

"We don't have much of a choice," I said. Bess

and George glanced at each other, and George nodded grimly.

"Let's get started, whatever this is," she said. "They want to challenge me on a computer? Bring it."

I nodded and sat down in the chair. My friends moved up to the front row and settled in the chairs on either side of me.

Using the keyboard and mouse attached to the chair, I logged in as VirtualNancy and entered my password. Within seconds, VirtualNancy appeared in front of her apartment, looking much happier and more refreshed than I was feeling at the moment.

She turned to the left, and I jumped as two strangers filled up the screen.

Well, strangers in that VirtualNancy had never met them before.

But they looked an awful lot like Robert Sung and Jack Crilley.

CYBERBULLIES

"That's them, isn't it?" breathed Bess at the same time George murmured, "Oh, wow." The two strange avatars advanced on VirtualNancy. I stiffened in my seat.

"It's the craziest thing," I told Bess and George. "I want to run away from them! But I guess that wouldn't solve anything."

George nodded, unable to tear her eyes away from the screen. The two figures hovered ominously, bobbing up and down and making odd gestures the way idle avatars do.

I directed VirtualNancy to wave and say "Hello." Immediately, the avatar on the left—the one that resembled Jack Crilley—responded.

KINGCRILLEY: VIRTUALNANCY. IT'S NICE TO BE SPEAKING
WITH YOU FINALLY, INSTEAD OF YOUR USELESS FRIENDS
AND BOYFRIEND.

I gasped. I felt like ice was running through my veins. "Does that mean . . ."

George's jaw had dropped. "They're UrNew-Reality," she whispered. "This whole time, it's been them!"

Bess shook her head. "But . . . but . . ."

"It makes perfect sense," George continued, her eyes lighting up with the realization. "I've said all along that UrNewReality had to be a serious hacker—how else would he or she be able to manipulate the game so well, and break so many of the rules? How would they be able to keep that creepy old-man avatar alive in that dingy apartment?"

I nodded. "It would be really easy if you had programmed the game in the first place."

Bess still looked stunned. "Wow. *Wow*. But does that mean . . ."

The Robert Sung avatar suddenly "spoke" to VirtualNancy.

SONGSUNGBLUE: LET'S NOT BEAT AROUND THE BUSH. IN
CASE YOU HAVEN'T FIGURED IT OUT ALREADY, WE WANT

YOU TO STOP HARASSING US AND DEFAMING OUR GAME.
WE HAVE YOUR BOYFRIEND.

I stopped reading after only a couple lines. "Oh my gosh. They have Ned!"

Bess nodded grimly. "And that's not all, Nance."

George shook her head. "It's definitely not all. Keep reading, Nance—they want to do battle with us *in the game*."

I scanned the rest of the message.

WE'LL MAKE A DEAL WITH YOU: IF YOU CAN FIND US
AND STOP US IN THE GAME, WE'LL SET NED FREE,
AND ONLY YOU WILL HAVE TO PAY THE PRICE FOR YOUR
MEDDLING.

"But—but—that's not fair!"

"It sure as heck isn't," George agreed. "They *designed* the game."

I started typing as quickly as I could.

VIRTUALNANCY: OF COURSE I'M WILLING TO WORK WITH
YOU TO GET NED BACK—BUT STOP YOU IN THE GAME?!
YOU PROGRAMMED THE GAME, ISN'T THAT A LITTLE
UNFAIR?

Both avatars dissolved into virtual laughter.

KINGCRILLEY: IT'S CUTE HOW YOU THINK YOU HAVE A
CHOICE, NANCY. I SUPPOSE I SHOULDN'T BE SURPRISED
THAT SUCH A SELF-RIGHTEOUS LITTLE TEENYBOPPER
WOULD HAVE TROUBLE FOLLOWING DIRECTIONS. WE TRIED
TO TELL YOU VERY CLEARLY TO MIND YOUR OWN BUSINESS
AND GIVE UP THE CASE, BUT DID YOU? NOOOO . . . AND
NOW POOR LITTLE NED WILL HAVE TO SUFFER.

I swallowed. Shaking now, I typed:

VIRTUALNANCY: DON'T HURT HIM.

The avatars laughed again.

SONGSUNGBLUE: IF YOU PLAY YOUR CARDS RIGHT, WE
WON'T HAVE TO. BUT LET'S MAKE A FEW THINGS CLEAR.
YOU MAY HAVE REALIZED THERE ARE CERTAIN . . .
THINGS TO BE DESIRED IN BETTERLIFE'S SECURITY
FEATURES.

"That's the understatement of the century,"
George muttered.

Bess stood up. "Keep him talking, Nancy," she
instructed me. "I don't seem to get any service
in here on my phone. I'm going to look for a
landline, an intercom, anything—there has to be

some way to get in touch with the police and tell them we're here."

"That's great," I agreed, "but I wish we knew where Ned is."

George stood as well. "I'll help," she said. "Try to keep them talking for as long as possible. Maybe that will give us some clues. Once you start the game and lose, I guess . . ."

"We're out of luck," I finished for her.

I began typing again.

VIRTUALNANCY: THE SECURITY PROBLEMS I FOUND WERE A SERIOUS ISSUE. THEY WERE HELPING A YOUNG GIRL BE BULLIED! AND THEN PEOPLE WERE USING THE GAME TO BULLY ME!

Onscreen, Crilley's avatar smirked.

KINGCRILLEY: WE WERE USING THE GAME TO BULLY YOU, SWEETHEART.

I shivered, feeling a sudden chill.

VIRTUALNANCY: AND SHANNON? IBRAHIM? NED? IT WAS YOU TWO WHO INVADED THEIR PERSONAL COMPUTERS AND E-MAILS, TRYING TO BLACKMAIL THEM?

Crilley's avatar shrugged.

KINGCRILLEY: SINCE YOU'RE GOING TO DECIDE TO KEEP
QUIET SOON, WHETHER YOU'RE SUCCESSFUL IN FREEING
YOUR BOYFRIEND OR NOT, I'LL LET YOU IN ON SOMETHING.

The avatar paused and leaned closer to Virtual-
Nancy, his pale, freckled, oddly young face taking
up most of the screen.

KINGCRILLEY: WE CAN GET INTO ALL THE COMPUTERS
AND E-MAILS. THE BETTERLIFE PROGRAM OVERRIDES
YOUR COMPUTER'S PALTRY SECURITY FEATURES. WE
KNOW ALL ABOUT YOUR ONLINE PURCHASES, NANCE,
AND WE READ ALL THE PAPERS YOU WROTE FOR MRS.
CUNNINGHAM'S ENGLISH CLASS.

I shivered again. I'd known someone had access
to my personal files, but still—the thought of
anyone going through my writings and Internet
history made me queasy.

Sung's avatar was laughing now. At first, I could
only hear the tinny electronic sound, but then the
screen expanded to show Sung's round, laughing face behind Crilley's. The two-dimensional
character was laughing so hard he was turning
red.

SONGSUNGBLUE: THAT'S WHY IT'S RIDICULOUS FOR YOU
TO THINK YOU CAN BEAT US, NANCY. WE'RE PROGRAMMING
GENIUSES. WE HAVE ACCESS TO THE PRIVATE FILES OF
MILLIONS OF AMERICANS——NOT THAT WE USE IT ALL.

I gulped.

VIRTUALNANCY: SO YOU DIDN'T CREATE YOUR PROGRAM
FOR MONEY, YOU CREATED IT TO SNOOP?

Crilley nodded.

KINGCRILLEY: WE CREATED IT FOR BOTH, ACTUALLY.
MAINLY BETTERLIFE IS JUST WHAT WE SAY IT IS: A
VIRTUAL REALITY COMMUNITY FOR PEOPLE TO SOCIALIZE
AND LIVE OUT THEIR FANTASIES. BUT IT'S ALSO A WAY
FOR US TO GET EVEN WITH PEOPLE WHO'VE WRONGED
US. THAT CHEERLEADER WHO POSTED MY LOVE NOTE ON
THE CLASS BULLETIN BOARD IN EIGHTH GRADE? SHE WAS
SURPRISED TO GET A NOTE FROM ME WITH AN E-MAIL TO
HER SECRET BOYFRIEND ATTACHED——ESPECIALLY WHEN I
THREATENED TO FORWARD IT TO HER HUSBAND.

I couldn't believe it. How long had this been
going on? How many people had Sung and Crilley contacted, threatening to expose their most
personal secrets?

VIRTUALNANCY: WHAT DID YOU WANT HER TO DO?
KINGCRILLEY: HUMILIATING THINGS, MOSTLY. I HAD
HER COME WASH MY CAR. I HAD HER WRITE A
LETTER TO THE TOWN PAPER ABOUT HOW BRILLIANT
A PROGRAM BETTERLIFE WAS, AND HOW THE WHOLE
TOWN SHOULD SIGN UP, AND HOW DARNED
ATTRACTIVE THE PROGRAMMERS ARE.

Yuck. Were these programmers still in junior high?

VIRTUALNANCY: DID SHE DO IT?
KINGCRILLEY: SHE DID. MOST OF THEM DO. WE HAVE
HUNDREDS OF "SLAVES" OUT THERE——THAT'S WHAT
WE CALL THEM——PEOPLE WILLING TO DO ANYTHING FOR
URNEWREALITY, JUST TO PREVENT HIM FROM TELLING
THEIR SECRETS.

This was incredible. A sudden thought occurred to me.

VIRTUALNANCY: THE GIRL WHO FELL IN THE LIBRARY?

Sung's avatar laughed again.

SONGSUNGBLUE: HAS A THING FOR BAD BOYS. RIGHT
NOW SHE'S SEEING A BOY HER PARENTS ASKED HER

TO BREAK UP WITH AFTER HE WAS ARRESTED FOR
SHOPLIFTING. BUT GUESS WHO HAS PHOTOS OF THE
TWO OF THEM CANOODLING AT THE MOVIES JUST LAST
WEEKEND? IT'S AMAZING WHAT COMPUTERS CAN TELL
YOU. . . .

I was stunned. I couldn't believe this. How
many people in River Heights were counted
among Sung and Crilley's "slaves"? It seemed
you had to upset them in some way for them to
go after you—as I had, by questioning their security, or as countless others probably had during
the duo's childhoods. But still—what an incredible violation of their users' privacy! And all for
what? So they could feel more powerful?

"Are you having any luck?" I called to Bess
and George.

"Nothing," Bess replied with a sigh.

George agreed, "I got that one text message,
but now I can't seem to get any service at all.
And there's no landline in here. There *is* a computer on the wall. . . ."

I stared at the huge images of Sung and Crilley
onscreen, still laughing and patting each other
on the back. What were these clowns planning to
do to Ned? "Can you try e-mailing the police?"
I asked.

George sighed. I heard her walking across the room, to what I assumed was the computer. "I can try," she replied glumly. "But we've seen how familiar they are with e-mail and the Internet this week. I can tell them we're trapped in the Gaming Garage. But who knows where Sung and Crilley are, and where they've taken Ned?"

As she began clicking and typing, Sung and Crilley seemed to remember their original plan.

KINGCRILLEY: ENOUGH BEATING AROUND THE BUSH. WE'RE PLAYING FOR YOUR BOYFRIEND'S FREEDOM HERE. EITHER WAY, YOU'RE GOING TO SHUT UP ABOUT OUR SECURITY ISSUES, OR I GUARANTEE YOU'LL REGRET IT. HOW MUCH YOU REGRET IT DEPENDS ON HOW YOU DO IN THIS GAME. IT COULD COST YOU A LITTLE TIME AND YOUR DIGNITY, OR IT COULD COST YOU YOUR BOYFRIEND. . . .

SONGSUNGBLUE: SO CATCH US, AND STOP US SOMEHOW, OR YOU WON'T SEE NED AGAIN.

I swallowed. I tried to imagine Ned with these two, tied up, hungry, probably scared out of his wits—but I couldn't complete the scenario in my mind, it made me too upset. I had to focus on beating these guys. That was, after all, the only chance I had of getting Ned out of there.

In the game, Sung and Crilley suddenly darted away from Nancy and began running down the street that led downtown. They were plowing ahead, knocking over shrubs, dogs, people—they even knocked over a virtual baby carriage in their hurry to get out of VirtualNancy's apartment complex. With a sigh, I directed VirtualNancy to follow them—just as quickly, and just as rudely. I comforted myself with the knowledge that these were only *virtual* shrubs, dogs and people—and that their owners would surely be okay with my behavior if they knew my boyfriend's freedom was at stake.

"I e-mailed the RHPD," George announced, suddenly right behind my chair. "Now let's see if we can figure out where they are. . . ."

"If that's even possible," Bess added, stepping up to flank my other side. "Poor Ned. I hope he's all right!"

"I can't think about it," I replied, watching the screen as VirtualNancy trailed Sung and Crilley to the entrance of the Virtual River Heights Mall. "Oh, no," I breathed as they entered, plowing down countless innocent shoppers as they ran. "This is going to get ugly."

"They're destroying their creation," Bess murmured, watching the action. "It's crazy. Sung and Crilley created this whole virtual world. Why would they want to hurt it?"

VirtualNancy chased SongSungBlue and King-Crilley down a long hallway, through a fountain (the onlookers were not amused), across the food court, and finally into the huge virtual bookstore she worked in. Sung and Crilley went to work, knocking over displays and shelving units. Books toppled everywhere, and many of the virtual customers were hurt. I couldn't let VirtualNancy stop, though; I had to keep her right on their trail, if I was to have even a chance of saving Ned.

AustensDaughter, the virtual shop's owner, screamed after VirtualNancy as she trailed Song-SungBlue and KingCrilley through the children's section, doing her best to avoid customers and fallen books.

AUSTENSDAUGHTER: NANCY! WHAT ON EARTH! HAVE YOU LOST YOUR MIND???

"Sorry," I whispered under my breath in real life. I had no time to even type the word into the keyboard. In fact, in the moment I'd taken to turn my attention to AustensDaughter—Virtual-Nancy had lost Sung and Crilley.

"What the—?" I sputtered in real life, searching the screen in front of me for any hint of an exit. I saw none. The children's section was encircled by low shelves, and VirtualNancy was blocking access to the entrance. The shelves were too high to jump over, and the section backed up onto a book-covered wall that looked completely solid to me. "Did you see where they went?" I asked Bess and George.

"No," Bess replied. "It's eerie! It's like they just disappeared into thin air."

George scowled. "Is it eerie, or is it cheating?" she asked. "Remember, they designed the game. It's entirely possible that they can give themselves powers VirtualNancy doesn't have."

I shook my head. "This is crazy. I guess I have to find an exit."

As VirtualNancy started searching the area, a loud, crashing sound filled the room—like cymbals. It was coming from the game.

"What was that?" Bess asked, standing up straight and staring at the screen.

George followed her gaze, searching the screen. "Oh, my gosh," she muttered, pointing to Virtual-Nancy's stats at the bottom of the screen. "Look!

VirtualNancy's strength just went down by a hundred points! And her hunger level skyrocketed!"

Just then, VirtualNancy's stomach rumbled in the game—loud enough for everyone in the bookstore to hear it.

"*That's* going to get annoying," Bess predicted.

"We don't have time to eat anything," I explained, directing VirtualNancy out of the bookstore and through an emergency exit out in the mall. "We have to catch them!"

"All right, that's it," George announced, and got up and walked over to the computer on the wall again.

"What are you doing?" I asked. VirtualNancy was stumbling from hunger, but I still managed to direct her through the parking lot. Finally, I spotted the virtual Sung and Crilley running down a street that led to Virtual River Heights downtown. I made VirtualNancy run after them, even though she was clearly feeling weak.

George was already typing away into an Internet browser. "I'm looking up cheat codes," she replied.

"Cheat codes?" Bess asked. "Are you telling me this whole time, all we've needed to cheat is a code?"

George shrugged. "It's not exactly considered

noble in the world of gaming to use cheat codes," she explained, "but it's sometimes necessary." She scowled at the computer. "Especially when we have to fight fire with fire."

"George," I said, as VirtualNancy panted after Sung and Crilley, "have you ever used cheat codes in this game before?"

George smiled and shook her head. "*Really,* Nance? Do you think VirtualNancy could afford that tricked-out computer I got her on *her* salary?"

Bess frowned. "Why didn't you get her some new clothes?"

George held up her hand. "Let's focus, here," she insisted. "Nancy, I want you to enter on the keyboard R-E-W-N-P-two hundred."

With no idea what I was actually doing, I followed George's directions. A happy sound, like a bell chiming, sounded instantly.

"Look!" Bess cried, pointing happily. "Your hunger level's back to normal!"

"Now type K-S-W-I-O five hundred," George instructed me. I did what she said.

The chime sounded again, and suddenly VirtualNancy's strength shot up by five hundred points. She was stronger than she'd ever been!

"George," I said as VirtualNancy chased Sung

and Crilley's avatars down Main Street, "do you have a code in there for catching two very badly behaved computer programmers?"

George smirked. "Negative," she responded. "But keep doing what you're doing. I'll try to help where I can."

As George and I joked, KingCrilley and Song-SungBlue approached a huge, wild-looking, magenta mansion that had been built just a few blocks from (virtual) downtown. The building looked nothing like any existing building in River Heights, but in BetterLife, the longer you played the game, the more power and money you accumulated. And with enough power and money, you could build the house of your dreams—even if that house looked too crazy to make it in the real world.

In fact, I realized as I directed VirtualNancy to follow them, I—or she, VirtualNancy—had been to this mansion before. A week or so ago, I'd been playing BetterLife and attended a party at this very mansion with some shady characters who eventually turned out to be the work of Shannon's aunt—and Ibrahim, who was just trying to get closer to me. I'm sad to say that for Virtual-Nancy, this party ended when she was tossed off the roof by the character Shannon's aunt had created. Bess, George, and I had been crushed. With hard work and determination, Bess and George had gotten VirtualNancy running again—but I was sure it hadn't been easy.

Bess frowned, apparently realizing the same thing I was. "Isn't this . . . ?"

"The site of VirtualNancy's demise?" I asked. "Yeah, it is."

"Do you think they know that?" George called from the computer. "Do you think they're trying to intimidate you?"

"If they are, it's not working," I replied, directing VirtualNancy up to the front door Crilley and Sung had just disappeared through. I directed her to push the door, and to my surprise, it swung right open.

"This is such an odd mansion," Bess muttered, watching the game.

"I know," I agreed. "I love the magenta paint job, the yellow trim, the big stained glass window with the eagle, and the towers." Two towers rose up from the mansion's roof—giving the whole place a purple palace sort of feel.

"It looks weirdly familiar, but I can't imagine where I would have seen it in real life," Bess continued.

"Yeah," I agreed. "I would think if you had

seen it somewhere, you would remember!"

Inside the mansion, chatter and laughter told me the rooms were filled with guests. Sung and Crilley had disappeared, but I directed Virtual-Nancy to walk down the front hall, peering into the rooms—and gasped at what I saw.

"That's Shannon's avatar," I said, pointing out a trendily-dressed blond teen on a sofa. "Blondie86! And—ohmigosh—that looks like the girl from the library!"

The girl who'd supposedly fallen off the ladder was holding a soda and talking to Shannon's avatar. Neither of them seemed to notice Virtual-Nancy as she poked her head out and moved on to the next room.

"Strangers," I murmured, taking in the chatting avatars. "Oh, wait! Ohmigosh! Look, it's Ibrahim!"

Ibrahim's avatar, BetterIbrahim4, was in a corner of the room chatting with a middle-aged lady, an older man with glasses, and a young girl of about thirteen. Again, no one noticed me peeking in, and I directed VirtualNancy out of the room before anyone spotted her.

"You know what this feels like, Nance," George said ominously.

"What?" I asked. "A very weird everyone-who-has-a-gripe-with-Nancy reunion?"

"Not quite," George replied, turning her focus back to the game, where VirtualNancy was climbing the stairs. "A gathering of all the 'slaves.'"

I swallowed hard as the full force of George's words hit me. *All the slaves.* It was true, Shannon, the girl in the library, and Ibrahim were all people UrNewReality had tried to blackmail—all people beholden to Sung and Crilley in some way. And the programmers had implied there were lots of "slaves" I didn't know. Could these strangers all be Sung and Crilley's playthings—people who did their bidding out of a fear of being found out?

"Why do you think Sung and Crilley would gather them all here?" I asked.

Bess shrugged. "What did they tell you you had to do to win, again?" she asked.

"*Stop* them," I replied. "At the time, I thought they meant physically—like a game of tag." I paused. "But now I wonder . . ."

"Maybe they want you to stop them from one final act of destruction," George suggested. "Remember how they were tearing up the mall. Maybe . . ."

"Ohmigosh," I said as it hit me. "Do you think they're going to try to do something to this house, with all these people in it?"

George shrugged, and my heart jumped into my throat. I knew that Virtual Sung and Crilley could only hurt virtual people—not Ibrahim and Shannon, but Ibrahim and Shannon's avatars. I had no idea whether Ibrahim and Shannon were actually playing BetterLife right now, or even knew that their avatars were attending this party. But ever since I'd created VirtualNancy and gotten turned on to BetterLife, the real world and the virtual world were becoming harder and harder to tell apart. My online problems had become my real-life problems. Who could say that, by hurting my friends' avatars, Sung and Crilley might not be planning to hurt them somehow in real life?

VirtualNancy charged up the stairs and began searching rooms on the second floor for any sign of the virtual programmers.

"Wait," said George, pointing to two desks in the corner of a room. "Look over there."

I made VirtualNancy approach the desks. They both held state-of-the-art computers, some photos, and some scattered papers. Above each computer, a diploma hung on the wall. Squinting to read them, I realized that they were both from Yale—one for "KingCrilley" and one for "SongSung-Blue."

"Robert Sung and Jack Crilley met at Yale," George explained. "I've read that in a million articles. They built a prototype of the game in their dorm's computer lab."

"Look at the photos," Bess suggested, leaning closer to the screen.

I made VirtualNancy zoom in on the photos. Sure enough, one desk held photos of KingCrilley with a pretty blond woman and a young boy. The other held photos of SongSungBlue with an Asian woman and two tiny babies.

"Robert Sung's wife gave birth to twins in March," George announced. "I read that in the same article. And in real life, Crilley has a son."

I nodded. "Which means . . ."

"This is their mansion," George replied. "At least, their virtual mansion. This isn't just some party house—they own it."

Just then, the cymbals sounded again, and Nancy's strength was depleted by three hundred points. She also lost all of her money in the blink of an eye. George groaned.

"Hold on," she advised me as I directed Virtual-Nancy out of the room. "Let me find the codes."

"It's funny that they don't just kill Virtual-Nancy," Bess observed, glancing at me with a shrug. "Right? They must have the power to do that."

"Yes, but if their behavior with the 'slaves' is any indication," I replied, "they just like playing with people. I think they're enjoying seeing me squirm, and trying to prove they're smarter than I am."

George found the codes to fix VirtualNancy's damage, and I began typing them in. Suddenly, Bess gasped and slapped her hand over her mouth.

"What is it?" I asked.

"I just remembered," she said, "where I remember this mansion from."

George snorted. "A nightmare?" she asked. "A nightmare where all the architecture was really obnoxious and over-the-top?"

Bess shook her head furiously. "It's not *exactly* this mansion. But it's similar. There's a big house a few miles outside of town on Glenn Road—you know, heading out toward farms and apple orchards."

I knew that area was pretty spread-out and

rural, but it had been years since I'd driven over there.

"It's not magenta, it's brown. And it's not *quite* this big—kind of a toned-down version of this." She paused. "But some really significant details are the same—like, it has two towers, Victorian-style. And it has a big stained glass window in front with an eagle."

I glanced at George—and I could tell we were both thinking the same thing. A stained glass window with an eagle? How common was that?

"Do you think it might be theirs?" I asked. "I mean, could that be where Sung or Crilley live in real life?"

George sighed. "I mean, I hadn't heard specifically that they live here," she said, "but it's definitely possible. I remember reading somewhere that Crilley lived in Chicago before college—so he might have family in the area."

"And that would explain why they're so buddy-buddy with Professor Frank," Bess added. "If they live here, they probably see each other all the time."

I shuddered. Poor Professor Frank. He hadn't been very nice to George and me the day before, but he was surely paying the price now—kidnapped by people he thought were his friends. I still wasn't sure how he, and his Guitarlvr15 avatar, played into the whole scenario with UrNew-Reality and Ned's kidnapping. But after the last few minutes, I believed it was a lot more complicated than I'd originally thought.

"Do you think—?" I began, almost too nervous to put my hopes into words. "Do you think that could be where they are? Where they're holding Ned?"

George nodded grimly. "I think it's definitely possible," she replied. "And I think it's worth an e-mail to the police."

I heard her typing as I tried to focus my attention back on the game. I had to find Sung and Crilley—VirtualNancy had to save all of her virtual friends in the mansion! Trying to think rationally, I had Nancy continue up to the bedrooms, searching every nook and cranny, even the closets. We found more strangers—more 'slaves', probably—but there was no sign of Crilley and Sung.

"That's it," I announced to Bess and George. "There are no more stairs. This is the top floor of the mansion, and they're not here."

Bess looked puzzled. "They have to be somewhere, Nance," she insisted. "Remember—Sung and Crilley created this game, and they have powers you don't. Could they have beamed themselves somewhere again?"

Well, that was a consideration. VirtualNancy scanned the room—and I noticed a small fire escape outside one of the bedroom windows. I made VirtualNancy check it out, and after opening the window and sticking her head out, she heard it—the telltale sign of Sung and Crilley's immature laughter.

It was coming from the roof.

"Do you have a 'get to the roof' code in there?" I asked George, hopefully.

George shook her head. "Sorry," she replied. "VirtualNancy is going to have to do this the old-fashioned way—climbing."

I sighed. I knew VirtualNancy was just an avatar, but I really didn't want to do her any harm and lose any chance of saving all of the virtual people chatting obliviously inside the mansion. Still, I moved VirtualNancy onto the fire escape, and had her look up at the roof.

"It won't be easy," Bess said, "but you can use the top of the window as a foothold. Then you can grab onto the gutter and pull yourself up."

I had VirtualNancy take a quick glance at the ground just as George shouted, "Don't look down!"

She was right. It was a long way—and I was terrified.

"Come on," Bess coaxed, "let's do this. Let's beat these boys and save these innocent people."

I nodded, swallowing and mustering all of my courage. Slowly, carefully, I directed Virtual-Nancy to climb up the outside of the mansion. Bess was right, VirtualNancy was able to use the top of the window as a foothold and grab the gutter. Unfortunately, when she did so, her feet came off the window trim, and she was dangling in space.

I tried frantically to get her to pull herself onto the roof by her arms, but she was too weak. "George!" I cried. "Quick! The strength cheat code!"

George read it off to me, and I quickly typed it into the keyboard, increasing Nancy's strength by seven hundred points. After that, she easily used her arms to pull herself onto the roof—even swinging around with the grace of an Olympic gymnast.

Sure enough, the programmers' avatars were on the roof, watching VirtualNancy struggle with virtual smirks.

SongSungBlue and KingCrilley fell silent as

VirtualNancy approached. KingCrilley smiled and, as VirtualNancy watched, pulled out a matchbook and carefully lit a match.

My heart jumped into my stomach.

KINGCRILLEY: WELL, I GUESS YOU CAUGHT UP WITH US, NANCY. CONGRATULATIONS—YOU'RE A MORE FORMIDABLE OPPONENT THAN WE THOUGHT.
SONGSUNGBLUE: AND YOU'RE JUST IN TIME . . .
KINGCRILLEY: TO WATCH US BURN THIS MANSION AND ALL OF OUR 'SLAVES' TO THE GROUND.

I gasped, pushing VirtualNancy forward.

VIRTUALNANCY: BUT WHY? WHY WOULD YOU WANT TO HURT THE PEOPLE WHO ALREADY DO WHATEVER YOU TELL THEM?

SongSungBlue smirked.

SONGSUNGBLUE: BECAUSE IT'S TIRESOME, NANCY. THESE PEOPLE DON'T CARE FOR US. THEY ONLY CARE THAT WE DON'T REVEAL THEIR SECRETS.
KINGCRILLEY: AND FRANKLY, THEY JUST DON'T SEEM WORTH THE EFFORT ANYMORE.
SONGSUNGBLUE: SO WE'RE GOING TO KILL THEM OFF IN

THE GAME——AND IN REAL LIFE, WE'LL JUST KILL THEIR
DIGNITY.
KINGCRILLEY: BY REVEALING THEIR SECRETS AT LAST.

I was stunned. Who knew how long Sung and
Crilley had been leading these people on, letting them do whatever they felt like in exchange
for supposedly keeping their secrets hidden? And
now they were going to reveal them all because
they were *bored*?

VIRTUALNANCY: YOU CAN'T DO THAT! STOP!

She ran across the roof toward them. SongSung-
Blue dropped his virtual match, and I directed
VirtualNancy to step on it, hard, extinguishing
the flame.

KINGCRILLEY: NICE TRY.

He lit another virtual match.

KINGCRILLEY: BUT WE DIDN'T BECOME VIRTUAL
MILLIONAIRES BY PLAYING BY THE RULES. BESIDES,
THE TIME IS RIGHT FOR CHANGE——WE DON'T WANT
RUMORS OF BLACKMAIL FOLLOWING US ONCE THE
SUBSCRIPTION PLAN IS RELEASED.

SONGSUNGBLUE: BETTER TO JUST BE DONE WITH IT ALL
RIGHT NOW.
KINGCRILLEY: AND BURN THIS PLACE TO THE GROUND.

I shivered. I knew that Crilley and Sung had
Ned and Professor Frank in real life. And they
were probably in a real-life mansion very similar
to this one. Could they—was it even possible—
were they considering burning their real-life
mansion too? And whoever remained inside?

VIRTUALNANCY: STOP! YOU CAN'T!
KINGCRILLEY: HA! WE CAN'T . . . WHAT? ACCESS
YOUR PERSONAL FILES? WE ALREADY DID. TAKE YOUR
BOYFRIEND? WE DID THAT, TOO.
SONGSUNGBLUE: YOU SHOULD STOP UNDERESTIMATING US.
VIRTUALNANCY: PLEASE . . . YOU CAN'T . . .

The second match dropped. This time, Virtual-
Nancy dove on it, smothering it beneath her
virtual foot. When she looked up, though, something had changed. Crilley and Sung were walking in circles, not focused on anything, making
odd hand gestures—the actions, I realized, of
unattended avatars.

VIRTUALNANCY: JACK? ROBERT?

A window popped up with a *bleep*.

KINGCRILLEY AND SONGSUNGBLUE ARE IDLE RIGHT NOW.
YOU MAY INTERACT WITH THEM WHEN THEIR OWNERS
RETURN TO THE GAME.

I glanced at George. "So—that means—"

"They left the computer," George replied. "For whatever reason."

I felt like this should be calming my nerves, but instead it just made me more nervous. Had they stepped away from the computer to light a real-life match? To hurt Ned or Professor Frank? To—

BEEP! BEEP! BEEP!

Another window had popped up.

SOMEONE IS TAPPING YOU ON THE SHOULDER.

I gasped and directed VirtualNancy to turn around. Had one of the guests downstairs followed me?

VirtualNancy's focus changed, and I cried out in relief as Ned's handsome, yet definitely not as handsome as real life, avatar filled my screen.

NATTYNED145: NANCY, ARE YOU ALL RIGHT? THE POLICE
ARE HERE! THEY SAID SOMETHING ABOUT RECEIVING AN
E-MAIL. . . .

Relief filled my whole body. I closed my eyes
and put my head in my hands, sighing deeply.
Just then, a knock sounded at the door.

"Anyone in there? This is the River Heights
police. We got an e-mail. . . ."

I glanced at George with a grin. "I guess they
do check their e-mail, after all."

"I guess they do," George agreed with a smile
and a nod. "I guess they really have joined the
twenty-first century."

BETTERBETTERLIFE

"**W**ell, I guess we're officially caught up," Ned told me with a smile as he grabbed the last bite of our tiramisu. It was a few nights later, and Ned and I were finally enjoying a real, relaxed date—without any unexpected interruptions or emergencies. It felt pretty nice.

"I guess so," I agreed. "How are students at the university responding to BetterLife going under?" Unfortunately for people like Shannon and Rebecca, the BetterLife subscription service was never unveiled—because its founders were arrested for kidnapping, harassment, and fraud just hours before it was scheduled to become available. After hearing of all the security lapses in BetterLife, the authorities had shut down the company and were debating whether to press charges against the hundred or so employees besides the founders. The security lapses were so huge, they reasoned—clearly Sung and Crilley weren't the only ones who had known about them.

Ned shrugged. "Oh, you know. Everyone was crushed, but then they just turned their attention to their Facebook profiles and their Twitter accounts. Technology moves so fast these days—it's only a matter of time before something new comes along to take BetterLife's place."

I nodded. "And you heard that PeopleSoft might be buying the BetterLife program?" I asked. "George says they want to make security upgrades and release it on their own. The money would go to Sung and Crilley's families—who apparently knew nothing about their shady dealings."

Ned nodded. "That would be nice," he said. "I have missed NattyNed145 a little bit."

I grinned. I didn't want to admit it, but sometimes I missed VirtualNancy, too.

"How's Professor Frank?" I asked. After questioning Sung and Crilley, the RHPD had found

Professor Frank completely innocent. It turned out he was a close friend of theirs, and he *had* invested $25,000 in the subscription plan, which he'd thought was genius. But he had no idea that his friends were using their brilliant software to collect personal information on users, or settle personal grudges. And Guitarlvr15—the avatar that had convinced the four of us that he was behind my cyberharassment—had been created on Frank's computer by one of Sung and Crilley's "slaves" at the university, at their direction. This "slave" had sent the messages to VirtualNancy to confuse me—Professor Frank had never been aware that his computer was involved in the transaction at all.

"He's okay," said Ned with a shrug. "A little shaken up by what happened. I could tell he never thought Sung and Crilley were capable of kidnapping."

Sung and Crilley had kept Ned and the professor together in Crilley's home on Glenn Road. I could still only imagine how scary it must have been for Ned and Professor Frank. I felt grateful every day that Bess had remembered the house, and our e-mail had worked—otherwise, who knew what might have happened to my boyfriend?

"And your dad's trial?" Ned asked, folding the

cash in with the check we'd split and pushing it to the end of the table, where the waitress would see it. "It's all going according to plan?"

"Yup, it starts Tuesday, and he's nervous, of course," I replied. "But only because it's a big case. The leaked files didn't end up hurting him at all."

"Good." Ned smiled, and stood from his chair. "Shall we head off to the festivities? I'm sure the al-Fulanis will want a chance to say good-bye."

I nodded cheerfully, and joined Ned on the short, chilly walk back to my Prius. Squeezing his hand, I unlocked the doors and got in, driving us back toward the center of town and Barbara's Beans, the cybercafe where this whole case had begun. The al-Fulanis were leaving tomorrow for Professor Al-Fulani's next assignment—they were all going to live in Hawaii for the next semester. Professor Al-Fulani would be a visiting professor of Peace Studies at the state university on Oahu.

At Barbara's Beans, cheerful music played over the din of what seemed like a hundred voices. "What a turnout!" I cried, surveying the amazing crowd. "It looks like half the town is here."

Ned nodded. "Well, the professor was super-popular at the university," he explained. "And after that whole incident at his lecture, I think a lot of students came out in support."

A few weeks ago, Professor Al-Fulani had been giving a lecture on peace that had been disrupted when an onlooker had claimed to see a laser pointing at his face—like a rifle scope. Ultimately, it all turned out to be a hoax perpetuated by Shannon's bigoted aunt, but it had still shaken the town.

Inside, we were consumed by the music and voices. I split off from Ned to go find Ibrahim. We'd been distant for the past few days, ever since the awkward scene in the pharmacy—but I truly had enjoyed getting to know him, and I wanted him to know that. I found him, finally, sitting with his sister at a small table, eating some good-bye cake.

"Hey there," I greeted the kids with a smile. "I just wanted to come over and say good-bye."

"Nancy!" Arij cried excitedly, jumping up to consume me in a big hug. "I'll miss you so much! Thank you for all the help you've given me!"

"No problem, Arij," I chuckled, hugging her back. "Enjoy Hawaii, okay? Tell the endangered sea turtles I say hello."

"I will." Arij leaned back and smiled at me. After a few seconds, something caught her eye and she was suddenly in motion again. "Oh! That's Emily from school! I'd better say goodbye to her. . . ."

As I watched with a smile, Arij disappeared into the crowd.

I turned back to Ibrahim, who looked quiet and awkward, poking his fork into his cake. Like at the pharmacy, toward the end of our conversation, he didn't seem to want to meet my eye.

"Ibrahim," I said softly. "I know things have been kind of strange between us lately. But I wanted to let you know, before you leave, how much I've truly enjoyed getting to know you and how much I'm going to miss you."

Ibrahim swallowed loudly, then looked up at me. He looked so confused—his dark eyes as wide and innocent as a puppy's. I wished I could take away the awkwardness.

"I loved getting to know you, too, Nancy," he replied, and I could hear the sincerity in his voice. "I wish things had been different at times. But I will truly miss you and think of you often."

I smiled, leaning in to give Ibrahim a quick hug. "Thank you," I said. "I really do appreciate that."

Ibrahim smiled shyly. "You really are a remarkable person, Nancy." He paused. "And I will always remember our time playing together on BetterLife!"

I laughed. "Me too!" I agreed. "Though some of that program, I wish I could forget."

We chatted and talked a little more, going over what had happened with Sung, Crilley, and BetterLife, as well as Ibrahim's plans and hopes for Hawaii. After a few minutes, Ibrahim was called away by a friend from school he had to say goodbye to. I gave him another hug, then wandered over to the computer area, where I spotted Bess and George.

"Hey!" Bess greeted me, smiling. "How was your date with Ned?"

"Nice," I replied with a relieved sigh. "It was really nice to just get to *talk* for a while, without having to worry about some silly case. How are you two?"

"Not bad," George replied. "This party is pretty hoppin'. Oh! I just remembered." She turned, suddenly, and brought up the Internet browser on one of the computers behind her.

"You know BetterLife is no more," I reminded her. "If you try to type in the URL, you just get a message that the site doesn't exist anymore."

George scowled. "I know that. Of course I know that. What I wanted to show you, Bess and

Nance—is a site *better* than BetterLife."

Bess glanced at me warily. "Better than Better-Life?" she asked. "What's it called—BetterBetter-Life?"

George shook her head, smiling in spite of herself. "*Better* than that," she said. "It's called PerfectLife."

Already, she had brought up the Login page of this PerfectLife program. It looked remarkably similar to BetterLife—so much so, in fact, I wondered if PeopleSoft would ever get around to relaunching that service. Things moved so fast on the Internet, as Ned has said earlier—by the time they were ready, perhaps six different virtual reality worlds would have already popped up to fill the void.

"It's a lot like BetterLife," George explained, "but—well, better. For example, you can watch everybody's activity, release arguments to the public and let them vote on them, create fantasy worlds . . ."

"Uh oh." I didn't realize that I was backing away from the computer until I ran into a table behind me.

"Don't you want to sign up?" George asked, turning to me imploringly. "We could resurrect VirtualNancy."

I cleared my throat. It was true, I missed VirtualNancy from time to time. Browsing in a (real-life) bookstore always made me think of her. And I'd recently added her early-on wardrobe back into my rotation: a blue sweater and khakis. Whenever I wore them, I felt a little, well, virtual—capable of more than your average Nancy Drew.

But the thought of joining another virtual reality world made my stomach flip. "No thanks," I told George. "I appreciate all the help you gave me . . . but I think I'm done with so-called Better Lives."

Bess smiled. "Well said," she added.

George shrugged. "Suit yourself," she replied, positioning the mouse over the Close button to close the Internet browser.

"Wait!" I cried, jumping forward and grabbing her hand. "Since we're here and all . . . and since you have the Internet up . . . I might as well check my e-mail."

CAROLYN KEENE

NANCY DREW

GIRL DETECTIVE

Secret Identity

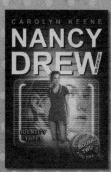
Identity Theft

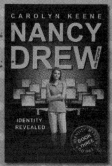
Identity Revealed

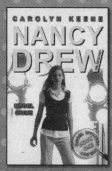
Model Crime

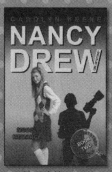
Model Menace

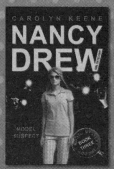
Model Suspect

INVESTIGATE THESE TWO THRILLING MYSTERY TRILOGIES!

FRANKLIN W. DIXON

THE HARDY BOYS

Undercover Brothers®

INVESTIGATE THESE TWO ADVENTUROUS MYSTERY TRILOGIES WITH AGENTS FRANK AND JOE HARDY!

#28 Galaxy X

#29 X-plosion

#31 Killer Mission

#32 Private Killer

#30 The X-Factor

#33 Killer Connections

From Aladdin
Published by Simon & Schuster